THE CLIQUE

ALSO
BY
BRANDIE

Don't Hate the Player

THE CLIQUE

BRANDIE

www.urbanbooks.net

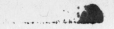

Urban Books
1199 Straight Path
West Babylon, NY 11704

ISBN-13: 978-1-60162-033-0
ISBN-10: 1-60162-033-0

First Printing February 2008
Printed in the United States of America

10 9 8 7 6 5 4 3 2 1

This is a work of fiction. Any references or similarities to actual events, real people, living, or dead, or to real locales are intended to give the novel a sense of reality. Any similarity to other names, characters, places, and incidents is entirely coincidental.

Submit Wholesale Orders to:
Kensington Publishing Corp.
C/O Penguin Group (USA) Inc.
Attention: Order Processing
405 Murray Hill Parkway
East Rutherford, NJ 07073-2316
Phone: 1-800-526-0275
Fax: 1-800-227-9604

Acknowledgments

Lord Jesus thank you for guiding me, allowing me to follow you on this journey called life. You have tested my strength, my heart, my will and my ability to remain sane. But I was and am ok with that because I know you are only making me a stronger soldier for your battle.

H.R.M., mommie loves you so much. But God loved you even more. Sweet boy there isn't a day that goes by that I don't look at your pictures or tell you I love you. Mommie will see you again.

AAAAAAHHHHHHH! This year has been pure hell. But I pulled through.

Thanks to Vera Layfield, you are such an inspiration, such a classy lady, loving and forgiving, so beautiful on the inside and out. God made you damn near perfect! I wish everyone could have a mother like you. I love you with all that I am!

William Rayford, my solid rock, my confidant, my extra back and ear, and the greatest daddie in the world. I love you so much. You have a wisdom that's untouchable. I appreciate every time I talk and see you. It's almost like looking in a mirror. I got you always! Love you.

Brandon Rayford, my best friend, and baby brother, even after the end. You are a positive force in my life. A true blessing. You will succeed in whatever you put your mind to. I always got your front, back, and side to side. I got you covered. KNOCK 'EM OUT!

D.J.—we have been through a hell of a time this year, losing our first child. But with us believing in God, he will pull us through this rough patch. Thank you for being the steel that held me together. Thank you for loving me unconditionally. I love you.

Bridgette Turner, we've grown up like sisters and been through every storm imaginable, but now it's time to let the sunshine in and complete this course called life. I love you, Kirra, Tyler, and Keith.

Jareka Butler, Girl you have grown up! I used to change your dirty diapers, now you're such a bright and beautiful young lady. And never let anyone steal your joy. You deserve the best and all that is good.

Baby Girl—Jerelene Lewis, Rona Lewis and Lisa Daniels, you women have had such a strong influence on who I am today. I love you. Grandma, Carrie Layfield-I love you.

Brenda Nash, thanks for being a great aunt and second mom.

Marcus from Nubian bookstore in Southlake Mall, thanks for being a vessel to my career.

To my clique of CLASSY LADIES—knowing your worth and expecting everyone else to know it too: Tracy Lias, Emily Davis Fowler, Lashonda Brock, Kanika Mosley, Latanya Frazier, Twanda Williams, Edith Weston, Treneka Hall, Tiffany Ellis, Jamila Cleveland,

To My Family: The Layfields, Rayfords, Mims, Butlers, Burks, Turners; love ya'll and thanks for always being there.

To all the people that believe in me, and are always a phone call away: My CSI clique, Evelyn Heath, Danette Jones, Barbara Jones, Ms. Pat, T-Bailey, Tasha Norwood, Jennifer, Adrian, and Ms. Margaret, and Ken Horsley and Cheche. And Xavier-thank you for reading my book and giving me pointers, New York representing.

Carla and Silas Harstfield—thank ya'll for always believing and caring for me.

Darius Lockwood, you are the truth, Darrel Jones, Mrs. Dora, Ms. Diane, Ms. Lesilie, Ms. Mary, Mr. Jones and Ms. Grace. To the NICU at Southern Regional and Scottish Rite crew, you all have no idea how much knowledge and comfort was given in two weeks. Thanks for all you did for my son.

Tim Roberts you're next!

URBAN family, thanks for putting me on the map. My next step with ya'll is to cover the Globe.

T.I.P, T.I., Clifford Harris, I'm looking for you. I wanna do a book with you!

To all my LOYAL readers, thank you, thank you, thank you, it's all for you. My unstable mind has caught up to my hand, and we are ready to commit murder on writers block and kick out back to back street books! Catch me brandietediebear@aol.com. Lord is Love.

CHAPTER 1

Tuesday morning June, 2005

R *ing, ring, ring!*
"He-ll-o," a sleepy voice answered.

"Bitch, put my muthafuckin' baby daddy on the phone!" the loud, angry woman demanded.

Mo swallowed hard, squinting her eyes together, trying to wake up out of the sound sleep she was in. She rose up, leaning on one elbow, glaring at the blue neon clock sitting on her nightstand. The time was 3:28 a.m.

"Funky bitch, you hear me? Put my baby daddy—"

Mo sighed loudly, taking the screaming voice in the phone away from her ear. *Here we go again,* she thought. *I'm so tired of this shit!* She cut her eyes to the right and watched Spencer—her and several other women's baby daddy—who was snoring like a pig.

"Bastard!" She mumbled to herself, as she reluctantly eased out of the bed and into the bathroom, where she could roast this hoe for interrupting her good sleep. She looked back at Spencer once more to make sure he was still sound asleep, closed the bathroom door, and took in a deep breath before letting loose. "Hoe, you callin' my mutha-fuckin' house, my phone, worrying about my man, my baby daddy. Hoe, ain't you sleepy, up all day and night worry-ing about a man that obviously occupying my bed?"

"You can kiss my ass! 'Cause if Spencer was yo man I wouldn't be carrying his baby."

That comment hit Mo in the gut. The screaming woman on the other end of the phone was right, and she probably was pregnant with his umpteenth child. She wanted to cry and yell, "Who is this? And why did he run to your bed?" But the ho was calling Mo's phone to prove something, so a challenge she was going to give her.

"I'm so tired of y'all lame-ass, wannabe-me hoes, claim-ing he got y'all pregnant or moved y'all into a condo, bought you a new car."

"Fuck you, ol' dumb, ghetto-ass bitch. Just put Spencer on this gotdamn phone!" The truth had struck a nerve with the irate woman.

Mo was on a roll, and she wasn't about to stop now. She was going to teach these bitches about fucking wit her. "Who is this? Cheryl? Kim? Lisa? Which stank pussy of the month is this?" She laughed, tickled to death that she was irritating the hell out of a woman who had intended to shake her up with the phone call .

"Yo' worst nightmare, bitch!"

"Obviously, I'm the one pressing on yo' mind. You calling me, knowing damn well Spencer got his own damn phone."

Mo had pulled the woman's card. The other end of the line went silent. It was clear that this woman had another agenda besides speaking with Spencer.

Feeling like she had one up on this hoochie, she sat down on the toilet, tired from the day before and from all the extra additives Spencer brought to their so-called "sea-soned" relationship.

"Well, since you don't believe shit stank, go look in the trunk of his silver Chevy. I left you a present." The deviant voice laughed, and the phone went dead.

Mo looked at her unfamiliar reflection in the chrome, circular mirror. She rubbed her fingers over her entire face and didn't recognize herself. Her once wide, bright eyes now had dark circles that made her look tired and worn out, older than her twenty-five years, all of this, compliments of trying to keep up with a whorish man.

I know this trick just trying to put fear in my heart and shake me up, but curiosity is getting the best of me. Against her better judgment she slipped on her light green, terry cloth robe, grabbed the keys to the Chevy, and remained barefoot to avoid turning on the lights and waking Spencer up. It was amazing that this man could sleep through dogs barking, telephones ringing, and a loud TV, but as soon as a light switched on, he was groaning and moaning for it to be turned off.

She lightly jogged down the stairs and out the front door, hesitating slightly to make sure no one else was outside with her, before stepping on the front porch. She popped the trunk with the remote. She threw a pair of sneakers, a tool kit, and a basketball to the side to find nothing. She knew Spencer's sneaky ass wouldn't leave anything behind. *Naw, not slick-ass Spencer. The only evidence he leaves behind is other bitches' babies.*

Ring, ring, ring!

She jumped, forgetting the phone was in the pocket of her robe. "Ain't shit in this trunk," Mo said, aggravated that she'd allowed some groupie to disturb her sleep and emotions.

"Oh, but it is, baby girl, it is. Look in the tool kit."

Mo snatched the kit and popped it open. She shook her head in disbelief. The sonogram read *Hye baby girl* and had a due date upcoming in two days.

CHAPTER 2

Mo shouldn't have been angry. This wasn't the first time Spencer had left behind a little surprise after he'd laid up with a sideline hoe. First, there was Pig, the neighborhood piece of ass. He said he was drunk and she took advantage of him. She took him all right, right to the delivery room and the courthouse.

Not even a week after Kaja was born, Sue's gold-digging ass knocked on the door with a pink bundle in her hand, claiming Spencer was her daughter Kendall's daddy. And all of this took place three years before Mo and Spencer had their first and only child, Kemoni.

Unfortunately, what was supposed to be the happiest day of Mo's life became one of the saddest. Down the hall from her hospital room, another young girl named Stacy had just given birth to Spencer's child, a stillborn.

Mo bit down hard on her bottom lip, letting the salty taste of blood settle into her mouth. She kept repeating the last name labeled in the corner of the sonogram. "Hye . . . Hye . . ."

"Yep. Mrs. Layla Hye to you, bitch."

Mo forgot she still had the phone tight in her hand, but the voice was no longer coming from the phone, it was coming from behind her. *I can't believe I let this ho creep up on me! Here I am digging in this damn trunk, not paying attention to my surroundings.*

With fear in her heart, not knowing if it was a gang of girls or a weapon waiting on her, Mo spun around on her bare feet and there was Layla.

Layla Hye was Mo's biggest rival, going back to the seventh grade. And now here they were still battling at age twenty-five.

Standing 5-9, all thick thighs and hips, Layla was badd. Her creamy, dark brown skin was flawless, and she looked like a gorgeous modern-day Amazon. The long eyelashes, perfect white teeth, and short, sleek, jet-black bob kept suitors at her door. But she didn't want just any suitor. Naw, she wanted Spencer Mack. And now, pregnant with his child, she had the assurance that he would be in her life forever.

With a nasty frown on her face, Mo said, "Damn, hoe, Spencer really got yo' ass sprung, riding up in front of my house at four in the morning." She began moving toward the street, where Layla was sitting in her car only a few feet from the entrance of the driveway. Mo felt a rush of heat run from her head to her toes. The anger running through her veins was enough to turn her into The Incredible Hulk.

Layla noticed the evil look on Mo's face. She thought she was too cute to fight, so she stayed locked tight in the '05 Mustang that Spencer purchased for her, with the window halfway down.

Layla was the classic dope man's bitch—obedient, spent all her money on designer clothes, kept up a lot of shit, and stayed in everybody else's business because she had no business about herself.

"Isn't she pretty? Looks just like her daddy." Layla was talking mad shit, her foot resting lightly on the gas pedal.

"Oh, you think having a baby by a hustler who already got countless baby mamas makes you special?" Mo searched the ground for an object to throw at Layla's smug face. "When you were childless, you was a hot commodity, but now you just a number, another one of Spencer's baby mamas."

"You just a baby mama, but I'm gon' be his wife." *Honkkkkkkkkk! Layla* blasted the loud horn. "Go get 'im so he can tell you that we gon' be together."

Mo laughed as she picked up a medium-sized rock. "Don't embarrass yourself. He'll do that for you in due time. Have you looking stupid, telling everybody that he leaving me and you and him gonna get married in Vegas and honeymoon in the Keys. Oh, and let me not forget the house in Lost Valley."

Layla's smile dropped. That's exactly what he'd told her, and what she'd been telling all her friends and family.

"Well, maybe this time I hit the jackpot, since yo' funky pussy can't get pregnant no more." Layla's smile returned. She knew that would knock Mo out faster than a punch could. "This good pussy can pop out as many as his heart desires. The boy you can never give him."

Mo was crushed. How could Spencer tell this trifling whore her deepest secret? She fumbled with the phone in her hand, making it recall Layla's number. When Layla looked down to retrieve the phone call, Mo chunked the first rock and hit her on the side of her head.

As the rock hit Layla's head, her foot came off the gas and clutch, and the car began to jerk.

Mo couldn't hold back any longer. The comment about her becoming sterile after Spencer gave her an STD was too much information for this trick. She threw the other rock, cracking the top of the window and sending shards of glass into Layla's eyes and mouth.

Layla screamed out, hitting the loud horn as she choked on small pieces of glass.

Mo rushed the car, pulling on the door handle and, at the same time, kicking the door, denting it with her bare heel. Mo reached into the broken window and grabbed hair, skin, anything she could get her hands on. When she finally got a hold of a handful of Layla's hair, she held on for dear life. The more Layla twisted and struggled to stay away, the harder Mo tried to pull her through the broken window.

"I bet . . . yo' ass . . . will think next . . . time . . . you step to . . . me!"

Layla was gagging as she tried to start the car, but she had a choice to make—fight Mo off and have a half a head of hair, or pull off and lose it all.

The glass began to cut into Moe's wrist and forearm as she tried to pull Layla's swollen, pregnant body through the window.

"Let me go. I'm pregnant," Layla yelled out.

"Mommy! Mommyyyyyyyyy!"

Mo instantly released Layla's hair and slowly backed away from the car.

Layla quickly started the Mustang and sped off, spitting glass, blood, and threats.

CHAPTER 3

The purple skyline presented itself to Royal as she slid her chocolate, silky, restless body from beneath her lover's arms. This had been the seventh night straight that her nightmare had woken her up at four-thirty in the morning, leaving her exhausted, black-eyed, and stressed out.

She walked her naked body into the kitchen and filled her ol' faithful, multi-colored mug with tea and vodka. As she sat at the table and gazed into the purple haze, she thought about the nightmare that was tearing her life apart.

Being the daughter of a dead, AIDS-infected mother and a deceased father, not to mention an evil stepmother, was a nightmare she'd dealt with, eyes wide open. Her best friend Mo would always tell her, "If you can go through everything that you've been through and still walk like yo shit don't stank, then you are my idol in every sense of the word."

Royal held her best friend's words in a chokehold.

❉   ❉   ❉

They'd met one hot, crazy summer when they were eight, in Newbie, Georgia. Royal, while on a time-out, sat behind a whitewashed wire fence on a huge peach porch, pouting and picking all the buds off her mother's white roses for revenge. Just then, a big silver car with a silver circle and *V* inside on the hood appeared, and a white lady and a little girl looking to be around the same age as Royal pulled up.

Royal thought, *Mrs. Busey must be taking in another foster kid.*

For about ten minutes, Royal made eye contact with the little light-skinned, almost white-looking, girl with dry, kinky hair across the street at Mrs. Busey's house. And she instantly wanted to go and play, but this stupid new time-out rule had her on lock.

Royal wasn't a bad child, just curious and rambunctious. But lately her mother had put her in time-out so much, it seemed her butt was beginning to flatten like a pancake from becoming best friends with the front porch. Her mother had become sick a few months earlier, and with every month some new symptom was claiming her body, and Royal's playtime.

After about thirty minutes of wishing, picking, and scooting across the porch, Mrs. Busey's front door busted open, and the white-looking girl ran like a slave across the street, not even looking to see if a car was coming. Royal would have to teach this new girl the codes of streets.

"Your ass will get run over if you don't look from side to side at least three times," Royal's mother would tell her whenever she took off a little too quickly.

The little girl rested her pale fingers on the wire and stared into Royal's eyes as if she was a monkey on display at the zoo.

Royal looked at the little girl's hands then at her own.

"Gosh, you are very, very black. My grandpa would say, 'Very berry,' " Pale said properly.

Royal laughed aloud then responded in her Southern dialect, "So what? You are confused, mixed up with black and white. Oreo!"

Pale shifted her weight from foot to foot. "I am white." She didn't care if the little girl she was looking at was orange. She just wanted to get out of that mean, old, fat lady's house that was yelling back and forth with her mother about a father she hadn't even met yet. But she was wondering if he was as dark as the pretty girl with gray eyes sitting in front of her.

"Not wit' dat nappy hair. And if you call me black again, I'm gon' come off this porch and whup yo' ass good."

The pale girl touched her hair like it was the first time she'd acknowledged it was on the top of her head.

At that very moment, the white lady fell out of Mrs. Busey's front door.

"Moses, Moses."

Mo was so caught up in running her fingers through the mess on top of her head, she didn't hear the lady calling her.

"Yo, DFACS lady callin' you."

DFACS? Mo would have to ask her grandfather what that was, since everyone she'd met that day kept throwing that word around.

As Mo was about to sprint back across the street, Royal ran to the fence. "My name Royal, since you gon' be stayin' at Mrs. Busey's house."

"I'm not staying at that fat lady's house. We just come to pick up my father," the girl answered.

As Mrs. Busey stood on the front porch in a pink, flowered duster, smoking a Newport and shouting obscenities, the white lady screamed to the top of her lungs, "Moses, let's go, dammit!"

As the girl ran back across the street without looking for any cars, She yelled, "My name is Mo!"

❁   ❁   ❁

Royal laughed to herself about the first of their many encounters before they became best friends. And now, after all they'd been through, Mo seemed to be at the heart her nightmares and heartache. She'd held on to her life-altering secret for eight long, hard years—for as long as she could—and now that she was about to turn twenty-five, she wanted to make things right in her life.

Her cousin Ascada told her that letting go and opening up would be the only way for God to forgive her and for her to move on to a prosperous future. Royal knew in her heart that all her troubles in life had come from keeping this secret. Maybe she would have to move out of the state of Georgia after revealing her secret to Mo. Maybe they could fight like two wild lionesses and then become cool again. Maybe.

CHAPTER 4

Mo finished wrapping the Ace bandage around her wrist and arm. She ran to her running car to check on a sleeping Kemoni one more time before heading back to deal with Spencer.

She first made a quick phone call to one of her best friends Emil, to let her know that she and her daughter would be there soon. She wanted to call Royal so bad, but lately it seemed like Royal was on another team.

Then Mo snuck back into the bedroom and straddled Spencer's thighs, pulling out his huge, already hard penis. She began to stroke him, rapidly rubbing the tip of his head with her thumb. Licking her thumb, drenching it with saliva, she returned it to the tip of his dick, moving it faster.

"Mmmmmm . . ."

Spencer tried to move, but Mo had his legs pinned. He continued to enjoy the strokes, thinking of Mo's juicy virgin-tight pussy. She was so good to him. She cooked all his favorite foods, ran his bath water after he'd come home from fucking other women. She even helped him keep track of all the child support payments he'd acquired while they were together, paying on time and adding two hundred extra dollars to keep the greedy mothers happy and off his back.

She was the mastermind behind the courier service that he'd started, delivering packages by flight and road trips, to launder his dope money. She was a blessing, and he planned to make her an honest woman. He had the five-carat rock in his safe, waiting for her birthday. He truly did love her.

His mother, Ms. Mack, told him time and time again, "You better hurry up and marry that sweet child. She the only one that put up with yo shit. And yo shit smell worse than hell."

And now here she was pleasing him, bringing him to his full potential for reasons other than pleasure.

Mo grimaced as Spencer moaned in pleasure. She glanced down at the bed, where she had placed her revenge—a soaked alcohol swab, the key to the house, and the Hye baby sonogram. She wished he'd hurry up and wake up, look her in the eyes, so she could get it all over with.

Why'd Mo stay with Spencer's trifling ass? Was it love, stupidity, dick-whipped, greed? It ran much deeper than that. He had her heart. She was fully aware of everything that was happening and what he was doing to her, but she owed him. He was there when her own mother turned her back on her.

CHAPTER 5

When Mo was fifteen years old, she got into some serious legal trouble that threatened to send her away for twenty years. As she sat nervously in the interrogation room waiting for the prosecutor to come in and read her all the charges, her young mind was in shambles as she thought about all the time she was facing. Spencer had reassured her that he had her back and that he wouldn't leave her side.

Mrs. Gabby Bravo, the young, blonde, blue-eyed, expensive-perfume-wearing, flawlessly made up prosecutor for the State of Georgia walked through the doors, a gleaming white smile on her face. She was escorted by two armed police officers. "Gentlemen, she's harmless. You can leave us."

As soon as their backs were turned, and they were out the door, her smile disappeared, and the face that Mo had always known appeared.

Without taking a seat, she said, "Moses, you are going to get rid of that bastard you are carrying, and that gorilla waiting outside."

Mo was shocked that, at a time like this, her mother would pull rank on her. "Are you serious?"

Gabby, a white woman with lots of power and no tolerance for what she called "ignorant, lazy, black folk," including the child she'd birthed, hit the table hard with her fist. "Hell, yes!" She began to pace the floor. "Without me, you will do a minimum of twenty years. And with me, those two things will not exist."

She stared at the mistake that she'd allowed her best friend to convince her to have because she said since the father was black the baby would come out with naturally curly hair and a permanent tan. How wrong she was, and how stupid Gabby was for having a baby for vanity.

Mo was considered light-skinned, almost white in the black community, but not light enough to pass for white, which Gabby desperately needed her to do. With all the success of becoming prosecutor, a new and respectable, wavy-haired, gray-eyed fiancé, and a perfect-white stepdaughter, she had no place in her life for fuck-ups. And that's exactly what was seated before her.

Gabby thought by sending Mo to Newbie, Georgia, a small city just outside of Atlanta, to stay with her father's mother for a year, she would identify with her black roots and know that's not how she wanted to live. But, no, she came back darker, pregnant, and in love with a thug.

"Noooo! Noooo!" Mo cried out. "I won't give up my baby."

"No? That's what I should have done to you, but I was too far along to get an abortion."

"Abortion." Mo said the word like it was brand-new to her vocabulary. "You can forget about it! Send me back to live with Grandma." She jumped out of her seat.

Her mother laughed wickedly. "Are you serious? You have five felony charges guaranteeing you twenty years. If your black ass doesn't get rid of them both, you'll do every bit of that time."

Mo yelled in her mother's face, "Fuck you!"

Gabby swung fast and fierce, her heavy fist plunging into Mo's stomach.

Mo, four months pregnant, immediately fell to her knees and held her cramping stomach.

Gabby squatted down to ear level with her. "You little disrespectful, ungrateful, black bitch. You are dead to me. I will do everything in my power to put you away for good, permanently out of my life. No more money, no more home, no more mother."

Mo didn't make eye contact with her mother. She just shook her head no.

Gabby stood up, straightened out her suit and spat on top of Mo's head. "Your life will be full of shit. I tried with you. I really did. Now you're on your own." She walked to the door without looking back at her broken-spirited daughter. "Guard, get me outta this room!"

In Mo's mind, all these things were apparent that hot summer day her mother dropped her off in Newbie to a grandmother she didn't know, with a small suitcase and thirty dollars, no explanation. She knew her evil mother was setting her up for failure, sending her straight into poverty. But she met a prince, and they fell in love.

Spencer was there for Mo every step of the way. He hit rock bottom, missed appointments with connects, let lucrative deals fall through, and went broke from spending all his savings on a top lawyer to get her off. He posted Mo's fifty-thousand-dollar bond, paid up her grandmother's bills for six months, and cried with her when she lost their baby boy.

❈   ❈   ❈

In court, Gabby tore Mo apart like she'd never changed her dirty diapers, or brought her into her teen years, showing her how to use tampons. But Mo's lawyer, smart and relentless, was worth every penny. He made the accusation that the prosecutor had personal motive against Mo and was angry with black people in general, because of her experience with her child's black father.

But the most damning evidence was that Gabby, as Mo's selfish, heartless, vindictive mother, drove her to the point of writing one hundred sixty-eight thousand dollars in bad checks, and identity theft.

Before Gabby's reputation and career could be ruined, she made a quick deal with the State on Mo's behalf. Part of the deal with Mo and her lawyer was that Mo had to sever her relationship with her mother, not acknowledge her in the courts, in the street, or on any kind of government documents.

Mo, never considering Gabby a mother anyway, hurriedly agreed.

And after all that hurt and confusion Mo believed Spencer when he promised to protect and care for her. But as she sat straddled on to of him, stroking his thick man hood, starring into his handsome face, she only saw the enemy.

"Damn, baby! You 'bout to make me nut. Sssssss!" Spencer said behind closed eyes, unaware of the real treat Mo was about to spring on him.

"Yeah, big daddy cum for me."

As she felt him thicken to his potential, she grabbed the sonogram, letting it dangle from her lips, and picked up the triple thick alcohol-soaked Q-Tip. She took a deep breath, one last look at Spencer's face, and swallowed the thick lump in her throat. It was finally going to be over.

Just as she felt him jerk, she stuck the alcohol-soaked Q-Tip in the pee-hole of his dick.

His eyes opened to the sonogram, and his body stiffened. More from the pain of seeing the sonogram and knowing that Mo was definitely leaving him than from the severe burning in his dick.

Mo was satisfied for the moment. She jumped out of the bed and ran down the stairs, through the open front door, and out of his life forever.

CHAPTER 6

Emil zoomed through her modest, hard-earned home, stepping over toys, shoes, and always, her husband's nasty drawers. She had a right mind to put all the doo-doo stained, holey pieces of underwear in a barrel and toast them. But he was a good man, a great provider, and wonderful father, even to the three that weren't his.

Emil shook her head at the clock that read 4:56 A.M., two hours earlier than when she'd usually wake up. Anything for her best friend. Mo had called and said she needed to stay for a couple days. She seemed to carry drama in her pockets and spent it freely.

Already tired before her day could begin, Emil let out a heavy sigh. Shit, her own life had just gotten heavier since she was suspended from the post office for stealing a seven-dollar book of stamps. Someone on her shift must have run out, took a book out of her drawer, and didn't account for it. And in government jobs, what's your responsibility will be your liability.

Now everything was going to be on Mekia's shoulders.

They were far from rich, a little bit over comfortable, and they couldn't afford one of them losing a good-paying job. And Emil couldn't get another job until the investigation was complete, which could take up to six months to a year.

What she needed to do was call that sorry-ass daddy of her second child, Lele's father, and threaten him with the po-po again. Dirty, triflin'-ass nigga. *He could walk around in Jordans, fresh haircuts, four-hundred-dollar outfits, feed hoes and their brats, but couldn't give his daughter fifty dollars for a pair of shoes.*

Her third child, T.J.'s father spoiled him and her. He was still in love with Emil and gave whatever she asked for T.J. She always ended up having to make it up to her other children so they wouldn't become jealous.

And then there was her precious Kaylen. Emil was attached, almost obsessive over Kaylen. Was it because she had her at the age of fourteen and grew up with her baby? Or was it because Kaylen was the product of her first love, Spencer?

That damn Spencer. Emil ran her soapy rag over her hairy mound down between her wet thighs.

Spencer was the love of her life. She was young, naïve, and hot in the pants. Spencer was Emil's brother's best friend and her worst nightmare. Her best friend Pepper tried to warn her, "Girl, I heard he ain't no good."

"Yo' young ass betta stop walking round here in them li'l-ass shawts, 'fore somebody get 'em." Spencer brushed past Emil.

"What? Yo' momma be the one to get 'em!"

And that was it. Three weeks later, Emil was with child. Her brother was furious and went after Spencer with a gun. They had a big fight that left Spencer with a limp that he perfected into a sexy dap.

Spencer spoiled Emil with oiled-down belly rubs, foot massages, and anything that she could stick in her mouth.

He loved the way a pregnant woman looked and felt. He would rub on her belly for hours, kissing and talking to it.

But once Kaylen was born, everything went to hell.

One hot summer day in July, Emil sat around for three hours waiting on Spencer to pick her and Kaylen up for his family picnic. She and her childhood friend Pepper sat on the bed playing with Kaylen.

Pepper saw the hurt in Emil's eyes as she called for the thirteenth time in ten minutes. On her last attempt, he finally answered the phone.

"Spencer, I thought you was coming to get us today?" Emil asked with an attitude.

"Us?"

"Yeah, muthafucka, *u-s*."

"Hey, hey. I ain't gon' sit on—"

"Fuck you!"

Emil yelled so loud, her mother ran into her room.

"N'all, folk. Fuck you, bitch!" He yelled into the phone.

"Bitch? Bitch?"

"Hang up the phone, Emil! Just hang it up!" her mother said.

Emil began to cry hysterically and jumped up, accidentally knocking Kaylen to the hardwood floor with a hard thud.

Kaylen let out a shrilling cry.

"What's wrong with my baby?" Spencer's voice became serious.

"Oh, shit!" Emil dropped the phone and retrieved her hurt daughter, kissing her bruised forehead.

Only a few minutes away from her house, Spencer was already on his way.

"Where my baby?" Spencer busted through the door. He snatched Kaylen out of Emil's arms.

Emil's mother jumped him from the back at the same

time Emil was pulling Kaylen's legs. "Oh, hell, n'all." And they all fell, with Kaylen's head being slammed to the floor for the second time.

"Nooooo!" Emil screamed as she gently lifted her baby into her arms.

Everyone was breathing hard, looking around at each other, trying to lay blame.

Emil kicked Spencer as she rose to her knees. "Look what you did, dirty fucka."

"I ain't gon' have this mess in my house, Emil. I'm too old for this shit!" Emil's mother crawled over to a rocking chair, clutching her heaving chest, and pulled herself into it.

As Emil kissed on Kaylen, her eyes began to roll into the back of her head. Her mouth tightened, and her skin became pale. "Momma, she ain't breathin!"

Her mother rushed over. "Stick yo finger in her mouth so she won't bite her tongue."

They rushed Kaylen to the hospital for what turned out to be a two-month stay. Doctors and DFACS workers rode their asses for the whole two months, saying that Kaylen's bruises—old bruises and scratches—were consistent with child abuse. But half of the scars she'd inflicted on herself, hitting herself in the lip with a toy. And once she fell off the bed at Spencer's mother's house.

But none of these explanations would do. DFACS took Kaylen and gave her to Emil's mother, but Emil couldn't live in the same house and had no visitation rights for three months.

Emil's mother agreed, took Kaylen in, and put Emil out. She treated the situation like a true foster care case, not letting Emil or Spencer's mother see Kaylen.

Her mother told her, "Maybe I can do a better job a second time around with my new daughter."

"New daughter?" Emil screamed, "That's my child."

"No, no, according to these DFACS papers she's mine."

"Fuck DFACS! That's my daughter!"

BAM! She hung up the phone on Emil.

Through the shared hurt of losing their child, Spencer and Emil moved in together. And that's when all the drama let loose and Emil found herself a true friend to the end.

CHAPTER 7

After two years of fighting, cussing, three abortions, and still no Kaylen back in their lives, Spencer and Emil decided that living together wasn't the right move. Emil moved in with Pepper and her money-hungry mother. Any price was good for Pepper's mother, even though she turned up her nose at Emil. As long as the price was right, anything went.

But the sexing never ceased, nor did her feelings for Spencer.

Ring, ring, ring!

This was the twenty-fifth time that Emil had called and left messages. Her mouth was dry, and her heart was flooded with the tears she was holding inside. She was the hard one in her friendship with Pepper, so she couldn't show her weakness.

Slam!

"Damn, don't break my phone over that nigga."

Emil jumped out of the bed. She pulled off her night-clothes and slipped into an all-black sweat suit.

Pepper was tired of all the scheming and game-playing that Emil was consistently doing, involving her as well. "What are you going to do now?"

"I know that muthafucka there. I just know it." She threw back the covers, looking for her black Reeboks.

"And what if he is? You gon' just bust up in his shit? And do what? Get knocked the fuck out?" Pepper adjusted her headscarf, folded her arms, and relaxed on her pillow. She refused to participate tonight.

Emil retrieved both their shoes, throwing Pepper's at her, "C'mon."

"It's one A.M. I ain't doin' this tonight. What about Kaylen, Emil? If you get caught fucking up, yo' momma got Kaylen for life."

Big tears about to fall, Emil looked at Pepper wide-eyed. "My baby is coming home, but . . . but I have to go and see if Spencer got somebody over there. I got to see for myself. Please, Pepper?"

Damn! Pepper knew she couldn't let her dawg go out at one A.M. by herself to her supposed-to-be nigga's house and definitely find some ho in his bed. Frustrated, Pepper threw the covers back, jumped up and grabbed her coat. Wearing only her pajamas, Pepper said, "C'mon, hoe, let's go. You owe me."

CHAPTER 8

Emil and Pepper got a ride from some neighborhood dope boys to Spencer and Emil's old apartment.

"I thought you said he let this place go and got the one in Ben Hill."

"He did, but for some reason I knew he lied about letting it go." Emil shook her head in disappointment, looking helpless, as they stooped behind a row of prickly bush.

"I swear—ouch!" Pepper looked at Emil. "Oh, I can't stand yo' ass."

They had been on stakeout for the last twenty minutes contemplating when to make their move. Even though Pepper was the scarier of the two, when she saw the three girls, she grabbed a sharp rock from the side of the building.

Emil's eyes were now thoroughly wet. She had seen Spencer come in with the white girl, along with her two friends, just as beautiful as she was. Seeing it in living color was like a knife through her heart.

"That dark-skinned girl looked real familiar. Like I went

to track camp with her. If she got hazel eyes, then her name is Royal."

"Royal?"

"Yeah. She pretty cool too. But she ain't from here. She from Newbie."

"And you don't know the white girl? Got all the information about the unimportant one, but the one with her stanking tongue down my baby daddy throat, you ain't got shit!"

Pepper didn't even respond to Emil's rudeness. She was used to it. If she wasn't telling Pepper how fat she was getting, she was criticizing the boyfriend of the moment or trying to tell her how to get her nagging money-hungry mother to go and shove it all up her fat ass.

Emil saw the light in the bedroom go on and then off. "Let's go."

"What? We gon just—"

Emil was gone, headed to the front door.

"Hold on," Pepper said out of breath. "At least go around to the back. You still got the key, right?"

When they entered the kitchen, they saw beer bottles, Crown Royal, purple sacks, dirty plates of rice, slimy noodles, and dried pizza that looked as if they'd been there for weeks.

Emil wiped the tears from her eyes. *He don't have any respect for our baby or me.* She peeped around the corner and saw the freaky, light eyes that Pepper had told her about. She had to come up with something quick before somebody came in the kitchen.

Chuck, Spencer's homeboy, was trying to mack on the thick, exotic-looking beauty to no avail. Emil understood. She'd smelled that hot-trash mouth of Chuck on too many occasions. The other girl was skinny and plain looking in the face, but looked like she rode a high horse from the way she was sitting in the chair with her legs properly crossed, and her fingertips barely touching the arms. And how she was sipping her juice. But the Fendi bag and shoes to match told the story.

"Y'all hoes sho get fat after y'all run track," Emil whispered to Pepper.

Pepper shot her a bird, thinking of a fat juicy steak and baked potato at that very moment. She wasn't generously fat, just thicker than her counterparts.

Emil took a deep breath and kissed the locket that held a picture of Kaylen, Spencer and herself. Pepper stayed on watch in the kitchen as Emil slipped through the door and down the hallway like a thief in the night, sneaking down the hall unnoticed because of the loud 50-inch TV.

She heard the girl's loud cries of passion coming through the door. That was her same noises, just last night.

Her heart thumped rapidly, too fast for her catch a breath. She just knew a heart attack was already in progress. She was waiting for her left arm to lock up and go numb. She put her hands on the door and slid to the floor, trying to catch her breath.

Spencer yelled, "Whose pussy is this, Mo?"

"Yours, daddy!"

"Tell me you want me in this wet ass."

"Oooh, yessssss, I want you in this good-ass pussy."

Emil gently twisted the knob, prepared to find the door locked and ready to kick it in, but it wasn't. She quietly entered the room and slowly moved toward the bed, where Mo's head was hanging off the edge. Emil gaped her legs open and slid over Mo's head.

Mo felt the presence of someone beside her and Spencer and opened her eyes.

Emil quickly clamped her legs closed, catching Mo's neck between her thighs.

Spencer yelled, "What the fuck!" He got up from the

bed, his dick swinging. He clothes-lined Emil in the throat, knocking her to the floor with a hard thud.

Mo scooted back on the bed, coughing and rubbing her throat.

Emil kicked and screamed like a wild woman. "You stupid bitch! Get outta my bed!" She wrestled loose and clawed at the sheets that were hanging on the edge of the bed, but Spencer caught her by the ankle and pulled her back.

"Let me go," she cried.

He pushed his fist into the middle of her back. "Stop it, Emil! Just stop it!"

"Your baby mama?" Mo asked, surprised and wide-eyed, clutching the same used green sheets Emil had come all over the night before.

Emil began laughing and crying at the same time, like a certified lunatic. "Yo' nasty ass couldn't even change the sheets."

"What?" Mo raised up out of the bed like the exorcist. "You fucked me on the same sheets y'all used?"

Spencer was speechless, and had that deer-in-the-headlights look.

Pepper heard the hard thud and knew her girl was in trouble. She ran past the girls, letting her presence be known.

"Was that a girl that just ran down the hall?" Ascada asked.

Royal jumped up and questioned Chuck. "What the hell is going on here?"

Chuck had seen Pepper run across the door, but he thought it was just the strong weed he'd smoked. "Ahhh, shit!" He took off down the hall behind her.

Everyone stopped in the doorway, mouths opened, eyes not believing what they were seeing.

Mo had Emil's head between her naked thighs as Emil

held tight to a handful of Mo's hair in one hand and was trying to crush Spencer's nuts in the other. They were all grunting and moaning in pain.

"This some real-girls-gone-wild shit." Chuck excitedly jumped around in a circle. "I need a camcorder for this!"

"Let her hair go." Royal began beating Emil on the hands.

Pepper quickly stepped in, knocking Royal into the wall, and all hell broke loose. Ascada's scaredy-bitch ass ran back to the living room and called the police.

Emil let go and jumped on Mo's naked body. If not for the true circumstances, this would have looked like top-notch girls gone wild.

Emil reeled back quick and punched Mo two times dead in the face. The blows blackened an eye and split a lip.

Mo reached out from behind closed eyes and scratched right above Emil's right eye down her cheek, leaving two long, deep wounds.

Pepper attempted to kick Royal while she was down, but Chuck jumped in front of her, taking the blow in the left shin. "Shit, bitch!"

Royal took a cheap shot and threw a strong punch to Pepper's temple, knocking her to the floor. But not before Pepper jabbed a sharp knife into Royal's neck.

Then the boys in blue busted through the door, guns drawn.

CHAPTER 9

The detective slammed down a stack of folders and a stale cup of coffee, spilling some onto the already-filthy table. "Somebody better start talking, or all y'all asses is going to the big house." He leaned back in the chair, exposing his beer belly. He squinted his eyes, stroked his beard, trying to seek out the weakest link.

Ascada Anderson, brought up in a privileged home, hadn't stopped crying since they put her in the back of the police car. She'd pleaded and begged with the young officer to just drop her off at home and she would pay him whatever, even with sex. He, in turn, told her he was now going to have to charge her with attempted bribery of an officer with lewd acts. Her mother was going to kill her.

The young officer said, "So, Miss Anderson, you are a prostitute?"

Ascada, snot running down her nose and her head in her lap, shook her head no. "I just wanna go home," she said, crying like a baby.

Mo, Emil, and Pepper stared at her in amazement. They

were all shook, but this chick was taking it to a whole 'nother level.

"Well, well, have these little hood rats given up who killed the girl?"

Ascada ran up to the detective. "Is my cousin dead?"

"You tell me, little miss proper. Is she?"

Ascada began to cry even harder, coughing and choking on her own spit.

"That big gaping hole in her neck wouldn't stop bleeding. She's in surgery now. The docs said it didn't look good. You little bitches are in a lot of trouble if that young lady dies."

Ascada fell out of her chair to the cold, dirty floor, rocking back and forth on her knees. "Noo, no, no. Please God, no!"

Mo jumped to her feet and stood in front of the detective. "Why don't you just stop? Leave her alone."

The detective walked up and Mo stared him down toe to toe. "Oh, so we got a live one."

Mo could smell the stale coffee and onion and sour cream chips on his dragon breath.

"What you gon' do, li'l wigger? You think hangin' with the hood rats gon' make you black?" He doubled over in laughter.

Pepper and Emil jumped to their feet to defend their honor.

Mo dug deep down inside her emotions. All the years of her mother's neglect and abuse festered into a closed fist. She punched the pudgy detective in the left jaw.

The short detective stumbled over Mo's chair, catching himself by his hands and knees. "Little bitch!"

As the detective gained his composure, he reached out to grab Mo's neck, but Emil was quicker, pushing the chair under him and making his stomach hit the bar of the chair hard. Then he fell to the floor on his hip with a cracking sound.

CHAPTER 10

One week and four days after the brawl at Spencer's and Emil's old apartment, and the fight at the police station with Detective Cantrell, all five girls sat at Walsh Juvenile Facility for girls. Hours after the attack, the detective persuaded the chief to send them to Walsh for jumping him and for stabbing Royal in the neck.

Once Royal was stitched up, she was shipped out to the custody of Atlanta PD for attacking one of the other girls. No officer could get any of the girls, except Ascada, to talk. And she confirmed both fights. Instead of giving her immunity as promised, Cantrell saw to it that all the "little black bitches" be sent to the nastiest, hardest, gang-infested girls facility in Georgia.

As the girls sat waiting anxiously for someone to rescue them, they had no choice but to "clique up" to survive. A gang of girls calling themselves Hood Bitches were hot on the asses of the new pretty girls from the ATL, especially the weakest link, Ascada.

Ascada couldn't hold down yet another trashy meal from Walsh's hell kitchen, so she rushed to the bathroom.

Tonk, the leader of the HB (Hood Bitches) had been watching and waiting every day, timing her, to see how long it took her to go and come back. This day nobody guarded her as she puked her guts out, so the leader made her move.

As Ascada hurried out of the bathroom and down the hallway, Tonk took another hallway and ended up on Ascada's heels before she could reach the cafeteria.

The tall, stout, gap-tooth, corn rowed, monstrous girl towered over Ascada. "You ready to give up ya juice, bitch?"

Nervously, Ascada moved close to the wall, but kept walking slowly. "I left it at the table."

Tonk jumped around and slapped the wall in front of Ascada's face, blocking her from walking.

Tears quickly dropped from her eyes. "Please . . . please don't—"

"Don't what, my new bitch?" Tonk got so close to Ascada's face, she could almost taste the rotten mystery meat that the facility served that day. "Coming in here actin' all cute like yo' shit don't stank. But I'm gon' find out if it do or not."

Ascada's five-foot, four-inch, one-hundred-pound-wet frame tried to slide by Tonk, but she pushed her heavy body into Ascada, mashing her into the wall. "You gon' give it, or am I gon' take it?"

The dead eyes staring into Ascada's was serious, horny, and fearless. Ascada figured she had nothing to lose. At that very moment, she understood that this big bear wanted to take her virgin pussy.

Tonk snatched opened the waist of Ascada's blue uniform with her left hand and stuck her other hand down Ascada's pants before she had time to protest. Her heavy body pressed Ascada's arms into the wall as she stuck two of her thick nasty fingers into her tight little pussy.

"No, no. Please!" Ascada protested.

"Bitch, if you get loud I'll cut yo' li'l-ass throat while you sleep." She dug her fingers deeper hitting her knuckles against Ascada's bone. She licked Ascada's pursed lips and tried to push her wet, slimy tongue into her mouth.

Pepper walked out the bathroom, trying to convince herself that she should call her greedy-ass mother to come and get her and Emil, but she knew it would cost more than she could afford. She could hear her mother now. *"I don't have no money for a goddamn lawyer. Y'all always in some shit. Maybe y'all need to sit down there for a while and get ya shit together."*

The money that her mother would cry about would be sitting in her fake coach bag and she'd be ready to spend it on booze, smokes, fishnets, wigs, mini skirts and young boyfriends.

What Pepper needed now was a prayer from up above. *If that Royal girl tell the police that I was the one that stabbed her then I'm looking at attempted murder charges. This is all Emil's fault. I told her dumb ass not to go over there in the first place. She had better find something incriminating to hold over her head.* Pepper choked back tears as she thought about all the time she was facing over stupid shit.

Pepper was almost back to the cafeteria, but slowed down because she heard what sounded like a puppy whimpering and a rough voice commanding. Since they'd been in lock up she'd been told of three rapes done by guards. The street in her told her to mind her business and keep on walking, but the curiosity in her wanted to see which guard she needed to stay away from.

Royal cut her eyes at Mo, who was sitting at the end of the table handcuffed to Emil. The first day they arrived at Walsh they got into another fight and, as punishment, were handcuffed together.

Mo mouthed the words, "What is wrong with you?"

But Royal turned her head away. She didn't understand the mean looks and nasty attitude Royal was throwing at her. Maybe she was mad that she was cut and blamed her for being there. But the evil eyes seemed deeper than that.

She and Mo had been friends since they were eight. And when Royal decided to move to Atlanta permanently, she ran into Mo at the mall and it was just like every other time. Sisterly.

Royal thought that moving to the ATL with her uncle, Ascada's father, would be the fresh new beginning she needed to survive her tortured past. So when Mo asked her to go out with her and the new love of her life, she was excited because she had her own surprise. But when Royal was late getting ready because of Ascada, Mo sent Chuck, one of Spencer's workers, to pick them up. And unfortunately for both of them there were all kinds of surprises let out of the bag that night.

CHAPTER 11

Royal looked at the small, silver clock on the gray, drab wall, in the huge dome-shaped room and noticed that Ascada had been gone over twenty minutes. She scanned the warehouse-looking cafeteria and accounted for every orange chair with a body wearing the same pale blue jail suit as she.

She came across the HB table and didn't see their mannish-looking leader. Royal knew she was there before Ascada left the table because she was yelling obscenities at them and the guard had to make her calm down.

Royal looked back to the end of the table, caught eyes with Mo and Emil, and then frantically jumped up from the table, snatching the fork from her plate and slipping it in her waistband.

She walked hastily up to the guard. "Bathroom," she said, grabbing her stomach like she had to shit.

"Go 'head. I done told these people that food gone kill y'all young ass before the street does."

Royal looked backed at the table once more, signaling Mo to come on.

Mo tried to jump up. "Come on, I got to go to the bathroom."

Emil stayed seated. She snatched Mo's arm back, pulling Mo back into her seat. "I'm not going no damn where. And you ain't got to go to no bathroom either. I saw her grab her fork. She goin' to save her little weak-ass cousin."

Mo squinted her eyes at Emil. "You saw that girl. You know she can't make it in here. And, by the way, where's your pretty, plump friend?"

Pepper had gotten into it with Tow of the HB on the first day they got to Walsh, but the guard saved her.

Emil looked over to the HB table and saw that Tonk and one of the other girls Pepper had gotten into it with were missing. "Let's go. I owe her."

"Damn! Yo' lil' pussy juicy and tight. I thank I'm gon' haf to take you in da bathroom and taste dis peach." Tonk overpowered Ascada, pushing her back toward the bathroom and never taking her hand out of her pants.

As they bent the corner, they bumped into Pepper.

"Shhhhh!" Tonk hissed. "Be quiet and go on 'bout yo' business and I'll make sure we cross you off our hit list."

Pepper watched Ascada's helpless eyes scream for help as Tonk pushed her into the bathroom. She truly felt bad for her.

"That's one big bitch. But God please look over me as I help someone who's as innocent in this mess as me."

Royal, Emil and Mo congregated in the hallway like they were at their high school discussing a good movie or book before the bell would ring for class. But this wasn't high school or fiction. This was very much the reality of life and death.

"Where are they?" Emil tried to listen for any kind of ruckus.

They only had enough time to check behind one door before the guards would be on their tails.

"They got to be in the east bathroom," Royal said nervously. "It wouldn't make sense for her to go any further."

"But Pepper would have come back to the table and said something," Emil said.

"Oh, she got nerve enough to stab me in the neck, but she ain't hard enough to help my little cousin?"

"That's my friend. Y'all are the enemy. I don't know why they just didn't handcuff y'all two hoes together anyway." Emil snatched the hand handcuffed to Mo, cutting into her wrist.

Just as the three of them were about to repeat what got them into this mess in the first place, they heard a loud thud and a shrilling scream. All three of the girls burst into the narrow bathroom, where Tonk was on top of Pepper in one of the stalls, choking her to death.

One of the mirrors was broke, and the glass lay tangled in the back of Tonk's hair. Ascada was in the corner crying, her pants down around her ankles.

Mo and Emil charged Tonk and snatched her off Pepper and dragged her out of the stall, and Pepper came up kicking Tonk in the face, knocking her to the floor.

Royal jumped up into the air and landed on her bloated stomach until she threw up a thick yellowish liquid.

"Ahhhhhhhhhh!" Tonk screamed, scared for her life.

"Shhhh!" Pepper put her fingers up to her lips. "If you be quiet we won't kill yo' big manly ass."

"Get over here," Emil ordered Ascada. "Give me that fork, Royal." She wanted Ascada to stab this butch to gain a reputation, and to have something over their head, so that Royal wouldn't be able to press charges on Pepper.

Ascada looked on wild-eyed and dazed. She didn't want any part of this crazy shit. She wanted Royal to never have come to live with them. She wanted to be laid up at home in her baby blue silk sheets that her father had shipped her from overseas, drinking sweet, hot cocoa, comparing her thin body to the models on the style channel.

Without hesitation or thinking of the consequences, Royal grabbed Ascada by the legs and dragged her over to the moaning Tonk. Royal pushed the fork into her hand. "Take care of this butch for raping you!"

"Do it, girl!" Mo yelled.

"Before somebody comes," Emil whispered, reeling Ascada in for payback.

Buzzzzzzzzzzz! The alarm sounded, alerting the guards to lock down the facility. They would be in the bathroom in a matter of minutes.

Pepper kneeled down, meeting Ascada eye to eye. "I helped you, and you were the enemy. But I did it for your safety. Nobody deserves what she was doing to you." Pepper was praying that this was her way to freedom. She reached out and squeezed the fork tight into Ascada's hand, pulling her to her bare knees. "Show the enemy that you have no fear."

Ascada trembled and hesitated as she looked at the big bull that had just raped her. She studied the faces of the girls who'd just saved her life.

"We don't know how long we gon' be here, Ascada. She will continue to rape—"

Ascada lunged at Tonk and dug the fork into her five times—the stomach, chest, arm, hand, and the tongue, the body parts she'd used to violate Ascada.

The other four girls put their hands in Tonk's blood and smeared it on their hands and clothes.

The door busted open, and the guns were drawn. The guards stared at the bloody massacre in disbelief. "What the hell . . ."

At that very moment, the five girls stood together and became known as "The Clique."

CHAPTER 12

July 2006

Three months after Mo alcohol-swabbed Spencer's penis and moved in with Emil, Spencer was withholding money from her, to persuade her to come back home.

They hadn't heard from Royal. She was on one of her disappearing acts, something she did every three months. Ascada was a newly-wed enjoying her new husband. And Pepper's controlling man of two years wasn't allowing her much contact with her so-called "low-class whores." He kept her busy in their million-dollar, high-rise condo, on shopping sprees, and extravagant vacations.

Emil walked into the living room and caught Mo daydreaming. "You ready, girl?"

"Nope," Mo sadly responded. Tears were forming, and she wasn't going to be able to stop them. "I don't want to go through with this. As bad as this hurts, I can't see myself with no one else." She rubbed her hands over her wet face. "I still love 'im."

"How Moses? Tell me how in the fuck do you love a

nigga that has all them kids on you, dates the one woman you hate most on earth, and cuts you and Kemoni off monetarily because he know you not working?" Emil shook her head from side to side, "Get cho ass up and let's go down here to this child support hearing."

When they entered the courthouse, Mo noticed a familiar-looking girl with an orange, spiked hairdo. She had twelve holes in her ear, one in her lip and eyebrow. The tight pink tank top with a dingy white bra strap peeking out, and jeans that would fit a four-year-old stood out like a sore thumb. If not for the new baby in the stroller she would have thought it was one of Spencer's baby mamas, Pig. But last she'd known, Pig had three school-age kids. She couldn't confirm it with Emil, who had gone to the bathroom.

As the spike-haired girl looked in Mo's direction, Mo hurried and turned the corner to enter the courtroom. She'd had encounters with Pig before, and if it was her, today would be no different.

As Mo walked down the aisle, she cringed at the many different races of men and women sitting divided in the courtroom. She didn't belong here. Never thought she would have to be there.

All the men sat up at attention at Mo's swinging hips. The Bebe shoes were pinching the hell out of her little toe, and she didn't have enough up top to fill out Emil's blouse, but she still made it work. When Mo met eyes with a few of them, they mouthed, "Hello. What's your number?" and even gave their numbers.

"No thanks. We're all here for the same reason," she said loud enough for them and their baby mamas to hear.

One in particular—he looked more groomed and sophisticated than the rest—made her do a double-take. His Cesar cut was full of neat, even waves, and he wore a tan and blue, pinstriped button-down shirt with a blue silk tie, showing off his broad shoulders. A Hermes briefcase sat on his thighs supporting a laptop waiting for his smooth big hands to punch its buttons.

Mo shook off her interest and noticed a beautiful white woman dressed sharply in an Akademiks velour suit. Maybe if she sat next to her she could find out where she got those red-and-silver huaraches.

Mo slid in the seat next to the beautiful woman. "Hi."

"Hi," the woman replied nicely.

Since being with Spencer, Mo had no acquaintances outside of the clique. It felt weird being cordial to another female without feeling threatened or having to defend herself.

"What's your number?" the slum voice asked.

Damn, she more street than we are. "Ahhmmm—"

Emil butted in as she slid down next to Mo. "They call you yet?"

"Naw. And I don't see him either." Mo looked around the room again, this time meeting eyes with the sophisticated brother. He nodded and gave her a sexy smile. She smiled back and continued scanning the room.

This time she locked eyes with the ragged orange-haired girl, and it was Pig. Pig licked her tongue at Mo and shot her the middle finger.

"My baby daddy ain't here yet either. I hope his ass don't come, so I can get all his money. 'Cause his other baby mamas ain't got him on child support."

Dismissing the young white girl, Mo's attention was focused on figuring out who Pig's new baby's daddy was. "What the fuck is she doing here?"

Emil looked around. "Who?"

"Don't look."

Emil twisted in her chair looking for familiar enemies.

"Don't look! You know that bitch love drama, and all she need is a little spark and she'll blow shit up."

"This place is stuffy, ain't?" The white girl unzipped the jacket of her sweat suit. "Oh, and my name Nevada."

Nevada had only been in Atlanta for six months and had not yet befriended anyone, but aggressive, freeloading, pussy-fiending men. These two girls seemed cool and spirited. And since they were in the same boat as she was, they at least had something in common.

"I'm Mo, and this is my sister Emil."

"Y'all sisters?" Nevada asked suspiciously. "I 'on't see no resemblance."

"Everybody ain't got the same mama and daddy or your ass wouldn't be down here talking 'bout being the first one to put yo' baby daddy on child support." Emil rolled her eyes at the young girl.

"All rise. Honorable Judge Cantrell presides."

CHAPTER 13

Neither Mo's nor Emil's legs would part with the hard steel flip chairs. Fear of the past, present, and future held them in a tight grip as Cantrell and Mo made eye contact. She instantly knew he wasn't giving her a dime.

"We gotta go." They both looked at each other to make the first move.

Just as they were about to sneak down the aisle and out the door, Spencer came through the door and dapped down the aisle, smooth and confident, his mother by his side.

"Shit!" Mo said, heading back to her seat." *I wish Pepper was here. She's so good with all this legal stuff.*

But before they made it back to their seat, the bailiff called out, "Case number 52422, to the podiums."

"Why you doin' this, Moses? You know Spencer loves you and takes good care of Kemoni, takes care of all his kids."

Tears fell from Mo's eyes. Ms. Mack had been her mother when her own mother disowned her. She knew Ms. Mack had her best interest at heart, but did her son?

"Come on home, Moses. Just come on home."

Emil took a seat on the front row, while Mo walked through the swing gate.

Nevada caught the gate before it closed. They looked into each other's questioning eyes. Pig twisted her bug-eyed, bright-weaved, over-accessorized, underdressed, stankin' ass down the aisle and through the gate like she was a runway model.

Mo looked wide-eyed and confused at Spencer, then over at Nevada and Pig, who was now standing next to her.

Nevada shrugged her shoulders, as if to say, "I'm sorry," and then mouthed the words, "I didn't know."

Pig sucked her teeth as she pushed her way to the front. "I'm ready, Ya Judge."

Cantrell shook his head at the disheveled, illiterate hood rat.

Mo's knees were weak, her stomach was upset, and she didn't know if her feet would be able to hold her up through this ordeal. She helplessly looked back at Emil.

Emil wore a confident face and a faint smile. "I got your back."

"State your case, Ms. . . ."

"Pig."

Cantrell laughed to himself. "Continue, Pytra."

Jovan Mims, the cutie pie with the sea of waves on his head and the ripple of muscles on his body, typed into his laptop. He noted that Cantrell seemed so unconcerned and disinterested in the young women's cases that he didn't even bother addressing them by their last name.

Loudly popping gum and talking fast, Pig said, "Well, all I want is my money for my kids." She held up two fingers.

Cantrell flipped through some papers, pretending he was looking for the sexes of Pig's children, but in fact, he'd already done his homework. He knew every baby mother and child back and forth. "And you have two girls with Mr. Mack?"

"Yeah. And he ain't gave me a dime in three months for Kaja." Pig didn't truly know if Kaya was Spencer's. He'd slipped her the dick one night when he was high and drunk, but he swore he'd worn a condom.

"Your Honor, I don't have but one child with Pytra," Spencer said.

Cantrell laughed like a jolly red-faced Santa on Christmas morning. It definitely wasn't Spencer's child, but Gabby and Cantrell had that fixed on legal documents.

"Well, son, on this DNA test, it shows ninety-nine point nine percent that Spencer Mack is the father."

"Hell naw!" Spencer yelled, feeling bamboozled.

As the courtroom erupted into laughter, shifting bodies, and crude comments, and Pig wore a million-dollar, gold-toothed smile, Cantrell banged his gavel several times. "Order in my courtroom! Young man, you are outta control. I will have no more of these outbursts."

Cantrell studied the hurt on Mo's face and marked that as his first blow to her gut. "Mr. Mack, your courier service brings in over eighty thousand dollars a month. And you have twenty-six employees at twelve to fifteen dollars an hour. So in the case of Kaja and Kaya, I'm ordering six fifty per child, per month."

"Hell yeah!" Pig jumped up in the air like she'd hit the lottery.

Cantrell hit his gavel. "Next, Nevada Ware."

Spencer gasped and wiped the sweat coming from his brow. He could handle that until he appealed Kaya's case. He looked at Nevada, but she wouldn't make eye contact with him. He knew she had his back. She wasn't like most girls.

Since everything had hit the fan with Mo, he'd slipped on their agreement, but she knew he would hit her back double.

CHAPTER 14

Nevada stepped to the podium nervously. She looked over at Spencer and then quickly looked away. She missed seeing his face, his company.

"State your first name and case."

"Nevada. I have a two-year-old daughter, Kamerion, with Spencer."

"Have you received anything from him since her birth?"

She looked out the corner of her eye at Spence and thought hard about the answer. She wanted to bolt and run out the door. Nevada swallowed hard and pushed the lie out of her mouth, "No, no, he hasn't given her anything."

"What the hell? Naw, y'all trippin' now!" Spencer began walking toward Nevada.

"Stop it, boy!" His mother, Ms. Mack, snatched his suit jacket. "You knew these triflin' girls were gon' turn on you. Now stand up for yourself and your kids and take it like a man."

Cantrell continued the damaging testimony. "Were you two in a serious relationship?"

"Yes. He told me . . . he told me that he loved me and then moved me and Kamerion from Florida to Atlanta so he could be closer to us."

Mo's eyes got big as saucers as she held on to her sick stomach.

Cantrell wanted to get on the floor and roll around laughing at the damage he was causing.

Weak knees and sick stomachs must have been contagious, because Spencer had caught both of them. Was it a conspiracy? "Mo, listen to me, I have never told nobody but you that I love you! I swear to God, I ain't never told nobody but you!" Spencer yelled out as his mother rubbed his back.

Cantrell beat his gavel like a crazy man to drown out Spencer's comment.

The intense eye contact that Spencer gave Mo told her that he might be telling the truth. He'd given Nevada fifteen hundred dollars a month. If he did one thing by his children, he financially took care of them.

"Order in my courtroom!" Cantrell pointed his gavel at Spencer. "Boy, you are only to speak to me!"

Nevada kept her eyes straight ahead on Cantrell, just as she'd been instructed.

"I see you've had a violent relationship with Spencer?"

"Yes sir, in May of two thousand five he jumped on me, and I called the police."

"Is this true, son?"

"No, Your Honor. She jumped on me, and when I attempted to leave her house, she called the police."

Spencer was being evasive, so that he wouldn't hurt Mo anymore than he had. But Cantrell wanted a fight, a straight-out street brawl.

"But they locked you up and charged you with domestic violence. In the report it says that you were shirtless and

Nevada wore your shirt." Cantrell looked at the expression on Mo's face and knew that was blow number two.

"Yes, sir. I was visiting my daughter, and . . . and she scraped her arm on the door and when the police—"

"Test proved one hundred percent paternity," Cantrell interrupted, not wanting Spencer to tell the whole story.

Then Mo would know that he was just visiting his daughter and Nevada got drunk and wanted him to have sex with her. But when he refused, she started a fight, called the police. And, once they got there, she scraped her arm on the door, and the police charged Spencer with abuse.

"Eight hundred dollars a month for Kamerion. Plus two years backpay at fifteen hundred a month."

Spencer grabbed his dick and took a swallow of air before he passed out. *I should put a hit out on these bitches. They know I take damn good care of my girls. Look at my baby over there. She look so out of place standing next to them chickenheads. She didn't have to come here. All she had to do was come home.*

Jovan Mims rubbed his chin, confused at what he was witnessing. He'd never seen a child support case conducted like this before. The sexy little woman he'd eyed earlier was up next. It almost seemed like Cantrell was salivating at the mouth for her case.

Just as Mo stepped to the podium, the court doors opened, and in walked Royal, Pepper, and Ascada, who was still honeymooning. They joined Emil on the front row.

All of them stared at Cantrell with ice-cold eyes, daring him to fuck with Mo.

Just in the knick of time, Mo turned around and spotted her clique. Blood began to flow through her veins again. She knew that something was fishy with this whole thing, especially since Cantrell was the judge. *The blood tests are probably fake. This bastard would do anything to bring me down.*

"Moses Whyte, prove your case."

Everyone in the court gasped. Jovan typed heavily into his computer. Even the bailiff looked strangely at Cantrell.

Spencer raised up and said, "She don't need to prove her case. I'd give her anything she ask for."

All the women in the courtroom oohed and ahhed, except Royal.

Cantrell jumped up and pointed his gavel at Spencer. "Boy, I warned you! Get outta here!" Cantrell screamed like a wild man.

No one in the court moved a muscle. Everyone was in shock at the action of the judge.

"Bailiff! Bailiff!" Cantrell limped breathlessly off his bench. "Get this mess outta my courtroom!"

The bailiff looked confused and unsure of what to do.

"Anything, Moses. I'll give it all up for you. Baby, I love you. Come—"

"Gotdamn it! Get him outta here! Hold him in contempt." Cantrell squeezed his chest. His breath was almost depleted. He sat back down in his chair. "Two hundred a month for the child in question."

Even though he was in severe pain, he took the time to wink at Mo, slammed his gavel, and left the courtroom for oxygen and pain medication.

The bailiff led Spencer out of the noisy courtroom. At times like these, Mo missed having a mother by her side.

Jovan grabbed his briefcase and rushed outside to call the station and report firsthand what just went down in Judge Robert Cantrell's courtroom.

Pig had left after The Clique walked in. She could handle one or two of them, but they always fought five up, and she couldn't handle them all.

Nevada began to realize that something was funny with this whole thing. When Gabby came to her house with the offer from Judge Cantrell, she'd known excessive information about Mo's life. Now she was feeling guilty. Had she done the right thing? Maybe she jumped the gun, wanting to get next to Spencer at any price.

CHAPTER 15

Pepper quickly turned the knob of her ten-thousand-square-foot penthouse that she shared with her Italian lover of almost three years. She didn't want any of his hired help to see her and report that she came in at three forty-five in the morning.

Holding her stilettos in one hand, she quickly and quietly closed the door with the other. Laying her face against the cold stainless steel door felt good to her tired jaw muscles and throat. She blew her breath into the air to release some of the tension in her throat.

An Italian accent came from the dark. "Got dick on your breath?"

Damn, this psycho is home. I thought he was still in Brazil. Shit!

Pepper pulled her white fitted dress down, running her hand over her thick, sexy body before she turned the lights on. She had a showcase with Grand Hustle Records, at club Kurical. She was that much closer to becoming a singer and able to move away from Joc. But she needed a few more months to finish shopping her demo around for the highest bidder.

"Turn the damn light off. I've seen enough," Joc demanded in a disgusted voice.

She could smell the liquor coming off his heated body. She turned the light back off and headed to her room. The moonlight from the skylight was enough to guide her to her bed.

"Whore." He slurred through a drunken tongue.

"What?"

Joc stood up, standing only a few inches taller than Pepper's five-six frame. "Ya look like a fuckin' street whore. From the long tangled hair, down to the slutty cheap white shoes."

Pepper was just about at her wits' end with this muthafucka. Yeah, the dick was good. Yeah, he was model gorgeous. And, yeah, he had endless money and properties. But was he sweet, caring, or tactful? *Everything has to be his way or the highway. I play by his rules, or he doesn't pay. I'm at his disposal, or the line to his wallet is cut and I'm thrown back into the free world.*

"So what you buy the eighteen-hundred-dollar Proenza Schouler's for, *J*, huh?" At times like these, she knew she made the wrong choice to leave Wisdom for Joc, leaving love for money.

Wisdom accepted Pepper in every way. When she was pudgy, he told her, "It's just more of you to love. You look good, baby." When she cried about making a C on her report card, he studied with her for the next semester, even though he was working and going to school himself. When her mother crushed her self-esteem, he was right there to piece her back together again.

Her mother would yell and torture her about being with a man who worked at Rally's. "What he gon' do, Pepper? Feed yo' fat ass until you pop. Throw you the pennies from his check. If you lay down with dogs, you gon' come up with fleas."

She listened to that noise day in and day out until his creamy, chocolate skin, deep dimples, fresh-smelling, supportive, loving arms, and sensitive nature weren't enough. And when Pepper's mother met Joc and introduced them, his money overshadowed everything she wanted in a man.

Joc choked back the last bit of his Patrón. "You like runnin' the streets with those sluts, don't you?"

Pepper was tired, and she wasn't having this conversation tonight. She cut her eyes at him and continued to walk toward her bedroom.

When he wanted to fuck the raw shit out of Pepper, to teach her a lesson, he sent her to the guest bedroom. "No. The guest bedroom."

"I'm going to bed, Joc." *Am I going to defy him and lose my monthly allowance? Why did I allow my money-hungry mother to set me up with this shark? I could have walked away after the first six months. After the first time he disrespected the shit out of me. And definitely after I found out he was part of the mafia.*

Joc threatened Pepper's life every other month, and he almost made good on his promise the first winter they spent together.

It was a Sunday night, and the football game was on. There was a house full of Joc's people, eating, drinking, and swearing. Pepper became tired and wanted to retire to bed for the evening. She kissed Joc on the cheek as she attempted to leave.

"Where are you off to?"

"I'm headed to bed, baby. I'm tired. I have a studio session early in the morning."

Joc roughly pulled her back down on the sofa. "You're fine." He patted her on the thigh like a good dog.

She stood again. "I said I'll see you in the morning."

This time Joc stood up. "So your crackin'-ass voice is more important than entertaining my family?"

Pepper had made him upset before, but this time, it seemed as if his pride was taking over. She began fidgeting with her hands. "I'm tired Joc. We've been—"

He threw his full cup of orange juice and gin in her face. "Take your sorry ass to bed! Everyone, say goodnight to the ungrateful whore. She's had enough of us common folk."

She was so outdone, she packed her bag and left undetected. After a couple of days of staying with her bitching mother and Joc constantly wooing her, she went back.

Joc made them a homemade Italian dinner by candlelight, red roses adorning every corner of the room, gave Pepper a mink, diamond necklace, and the twenty-two-hundred-dollar Devi Kroell clutch she'd been talking his head off about.

"I'm so glad to be home," Pepper said as they walked to their bedroom. She had to stop halfway down the hallway because she began to feel woozy, but dared not say that she wanted to go to bed, in fear of a repeat of game night.

"I'm going to show you just how much I missed you," Joc said in a devious voice.

And that's the last thing Pepper remembered when she woke up in the guest bedroom. Her head was pounding. She tried the bedroom door, but it was locked. She shook her head a few times before she realized that the bedroom was completely empty.

"What the fuck is going on?"

It looked like the same room, but without furniture. She tried to flick on the light, but there was no power. Her next attempt was the bathroom door, which was nailed shut. "That bastard." She pounded heavily on the door, screaming at the top of her lungs, "Joc, you bastard! Let me outta here. Joc!" She kicked the door, stubbing her toe. "Ouuuu! Joooooccc!"

Through tear-filled eyes, Pepper surveyed the bedroom. Joc had left five one-gallon jugs of water, an empty can that fit her ass perfectly, and a note. It read:

> *You think you can make it in this big old world by yourself. With a felony record, if you leave me, you will never get a job paying you enough to survive. Pepper, you will end up like this. Remember, I care for you and will always take care of you if you live by my means and my standards. All you have to do is follow the rules.*
> *I love you*

Joc slammed his glass down on the expensive, fragile, round, glass table, creating a lightening crack across it, imitating what his insides were feeling like. He walked past Pepper and unbuttoned his shirt. "Live by the rule, die by breaking it."

Pepper cried on the inside before she entered the lavish guest bedroom. The all-glass room used to freak Pepper out, until she learned to use the mirrors to her advantage. The huge crystal chandelier hung around the bed like a spider, with bars in between the strands of crystals for Pepper to hold on to.

Joc's sexy ass lay back on twenty goose down pillows like a pharaoh awaiting his sexy belly dancer to serenade him. He pressed two buttons on the digital remote. "Insatiable" by Prince blasted through the speakers. Then the lights dimmed, and he demanded in a sexy tone, "Dance."

Pepper loved the way he took control in the bedroom. That was her weakness—the money and the power. She stepped out of her expensive white dress and all of her self-respect.

As she climbed onto the bed he instructed her, "Slower."

Pepper slowed down, arching her back like a hungry cheetah about to strike her prey. She slowly wound her brown hips as she continued to crawl over to him.

Over the years Pepper's shorter, chubbier body had lengthened into a solid, luscious body of nonstop curves, all in the right places.

She stood over Joc, exposing her well-manicured valley of love.

Seeing her stand in the crystal shower turned him on. He sensually licked his first two fingers, slowly running them from the bottom of her stomach down to the straight hair that covered her sweet mound.

Pepper sucked in a deep breath to keep her composure. She continued to gyrate her hips, making her stomach move with a wave-like motion.

He couldn't take anymore. Just like Prince sang, "She was his living fantasy." And he wanted her untouched and fresh from the clutches of the dirty world. Her plump backside was now in his face. "Make it clap, baby."

She did exactly as he requested. Then he aggressively pulled her down into a squat.

First, he inhaled her sweet scent, rubbing his nose gently back and forth against the opening of her vagina. Then extending his tongue as he rubbed his nose, he pressed his full tongue back and forth against her clit.

"Daddy, please, give it to me." Pepper fell to her knees unable to hold strong. As she folded over, she positioned her knees by Joc's ears and lay forth into his lap, face first.

His rock-hard dick was ready for the taking. She slipped him into her mouth, without using her hands and pushed his thick stick to the back of her throat with her juicy, plump lips.

"Damn, baby!" Joc yelled out in pleasure, burying his nails into her hips.

Pepper grimaced at the pain, but continued pleasuring

Joc. She gently slid her teeth up to the head of his nine-inch dick, smoothing it with the tips of her thick, hungry lips. Grabbing a handful of dick, she folded her thick lips over the head of his dick and sucked hard on the opening of his penis.

"Ahhhh, mama! You gon' make me nut in yo' wet-ass mouth."

She lashed her tongue around and around, faster and faster, until he exploded in her mouth. She took it all down her deep sore throat, not spilling one drop.

"Pepper, girllll, you are the best!" Joc roughly pushed her onto her stomach, pushing himself to his knees in the transition. Joc snatched Pepper to her knees by the waist and tapped his healthy pole against her dripping pussy, making sure she was ready to take him.

Pepper's heart raced with excitement as he toyed with what he knew she wanted—all of him—her sensitive pussy pulsating like a beating heart.

He put the tip of the head in first, and her monster clung tight onto it. This was what he'd been missing the last week and a half in Brazil.

She pushed her full cushion back into him as far as she could before he worked the rest of his inches deep inside her. Pepper screamed out as Joc buried his snake deep into her pond.

When he hit rock bottom, they both screamed out in ecstasy. He fell into her plump ass.

She did some grinding, pasting her wetness onto his dick. "Ummm, daddy, make this pussy cum all over you."

He slightly raised her hips to the air and blocked her from coming down by sliding his knees under her. Then he bounced her ass like a pony at the fair.

"Joc . . . Joc . . . I love you." Pepper could hardly breathe. She held on tight to the sheets in fear she would go flying onto the floor.

Joc slapped both her ass cheeks and watched them bounce like Jell-O. "Take your dick, baby," he said in Italian, as he long-stroked her wet pussy. As he rubbed her sweaty back, he pushed her lower back down harder onto his pulsating dick.

Pepper clinched her pussy muscles tight as Joc slammed into her one last time before they both came and lay in each other's arms for a couple of minutes.

Then Joc said, "You can sleep in here tonight. You're on punishment." He patted Pepper on her bountiful ass and disappeared out the door.

Tonight Pepper didn't mind. That love that Joc just got out of her was full of memories of Wisdom. She wanted to sleep alone and dream about the man she truly loved and gave up for nothing. Maybe one day she'd run into him, and he would be able to forgive her. They would start just where they left off, get married, and have the son he always talked about. She smiled to herself and drifted off to a peaceful sleep.

CHAPTER 16

September 2006

It'd been only two months after the beautiful, immaculate wedding, yet twenty-three-year-old Ascada wore a heavy coat of burden, confusion, and uncertainty as she sat in front of her Sony 72-inch TV and watched Oprah move her lips, not hearing one word in spite of the loud volume. She'd always been known as weak and soft, but after the ordeal at Walsh, she grew balls and a sassy mouth.

At first it was hard for her to trust anyone, but after a little persuasion from her mother and Royal, she went out with one of Atlanta's biggest socialites, Hunter Cambell, the former mayor's playboy son. Every party Ascada attended, he was there. Every dinner table she sat at, so did he. She bumped into him so much that he finally knocked her down, literally and figuratively.

Everything happened so fast—the three dates, the meeting of families, the proposal, the marriage, and now, the infidelity.

BAM, BAM, BAM!

Ascada hated Royal's police knock. "Come in," she yelled from the couch, not wanting to move all the receipts and printed e-mails she'd found.

Royal rushed into the door, a fierce look on her face. "I can't believe this shit!"

"I know." Ascada held her head in her hands. "I can't either."

Royal put her hand on her hip and shook her head. "I'm going to kill that muthafuckin' bitch!"

"Thanks, but I don't want to go to jail again."

Royal was deep into her own thoughts, forgetting that her cousin had called her to come over and help her with her cheating husband. Royal threw a letter into Ascada's lap. It was stamped in bold red and read, *SSI RECOVERY DEPARTMENT.*

"What is this?"

"Bebe is the bitch I'm going to kill."

"Bebe? What she got to do with your SSI check?"

After Royal's mother died of AIDS when she was twelve, her father had married a mean, hateful woman named Bebe, with two kids of her own. She moved in and immediately made herself and her kids at home. Since Royal's father worked for the railroad, he was always gone and left his still tenderhearted children under the care of the conniving, sneaky Bebe.

"Get y'all asses up, and clean up, and cook breakfast," Bebe demanded at five-thirty one Saturday morning while her two fat lazy-ass whales of daughters slept, snoring like mules.

"Why can't Stefanie and Stacey help us?" Royal was on her knees scrubbing the bathroom with Comet.

Bebe squinted her eyes, walked over to Royal, and kicked her hard in the stomach, knocking her in the bathtub. She grabbed the Comet, stood over the young child, and put her foot on her neck. Then she doused half the Comet can into her mouth and eyes.

"If you ever question my authority, I will have my husband send yo' dingy black ass to an all-girls school. Do you understand me?"

Royal managed to squeeze out through Comet and small breaths of air. "Yes."

Bebe pushed down a little more. "Yes what, asshole?"

"Yes, ma'am."

Royal had several encounters with Bebe like this. She'd never told her dad because he looked so sick and preoccupied after her mother's death. And Bebe took full advantage of his being sad, hurt, and always away.

Once, when her father had come back from a three-week stint, Bebe had moved the family into a brand-new house. She put his three kids into the smallest bedrooms, while her girls had their own bedrooms. When her mother's SSI checks began coming in, she took all three of them out of the mail and deposited them into her account.

After Royal had endured a year of misery and abuse from her stepmother, her father was killed at work, on the railroad. And, once again, when the survivor benefits kicked in, Bebe took them too.

Living in Newbie, Georgia, Royal and her siblings were alone, all their family being in Atlanta and Florida. When Royal got pregnant at fifteen, Bebe treated her so bad, she ran away and stayed with her mother's best friend, who helped her stay in school, and apply for all the grants and free money a young black single mother going to school could get for two dead parents. Instead of just getting the two checks transferred to her new address, she applied for new ones, and Bebe continued to receive the old ones.

And now the SSI and the railroad were accusing Royal of fraud, claiming she had to pay back from the time she was fifteen—she was now twenty-four—and the college tuition that was paid, totaling three hundred, seventy-nine thousand dollars, or she would go to jail for ten years. What was she going to do? She'd never had a job because of her trumped-up record. The railroad and SSI continued to pay her because she was going to college. And now that she was in medical school, she definitely didn't have time to get a job. This money was her and King's only means.

She smiled when she thought about her lil' man, her little eight-year-old blessing that kept her sane. She would just have to get a lawyer and sue Bebe, make the government see what she'd done.

CHAPTER 17

Royal snapped out of her own thoughts and focused on Ascada's teary face as she sat on the butterscotch leather sectional surrounded by piles of what looked like bank statements, store receipts, and cell phone records. She pushed over a stack of papers and sat next to Ascada.

"I'm sorry, Scada. I ran up in your crib blasting off about my problems and you called me for a shoulder to lean on."

"That's all right. I'll help you find a lawyer."

"So what's mister perfect done?"

Ascada threw both her hands up. "I don't know yet." She picked up the phone record. "See, like this." She pointed to a repeat 678 number. "I just knew when I called it that it would be a woman."

"Why?"

"Because, look, he called at twelve one night, two A.M., three-sixteen A.M., four-twenty-three A.M., and a lot more during the day around lunchtime."

"Maybe it's business," Royal said, unconvinced.

"At three and four in the morning? No, I don't think so.

And look at these credit card receipts. When this phone number appears at lunchtime, twenty to thirty minutes later there is a charge from a boutique or a restaurant."

"Have you called the number?"

"Yeah, and a man answers."

"Well, ms. detective, did you ask him, is his wife cheating or does he have a sister or mother living there?"

"No," Ascada answered, thinking that's exactly why she called Royal's smart ass. She grabbed the phone and shoved it in Royal's hand. "Here, go for it."

Royal would do anything for Ascada because she felt responsible for getting her caught up in all that mess when they were teenagers.

Please, Lord, just let this be an overreacting new bride that thinks everyone wants her husband, because he chose her instead of them.

Royal dialed the number and let it ring five times. "No one's answering."

A soft voice answered, "Hello."

Royal was shocked. She didn't expect anyone to answer after all the rings, and she couldn't make a distinctive ID on the voice. "Ahhm, ma'am, I'm calling from Royalty Treasures out of New York, and I'm trying to confirm the right address for a delivery."

"A delivery? Ooh . . . what is it?"

"Umm, ma'am, I don't know. It's already boxed up, and the sender is sending it as secret admirer."

The more Royal talked to the person and listened to certain words, she confirmed that this was a man. So why was he letting her call him *ma'am*?

Ascada anxiously pulled on Royal's shirt. "What is she saying?"

"I wonder who's sending me a gift." The man popped his lips. "Well, the address is forty-eight ninety Cassell Way."

Royal heard his doorbell ring.

He immediately said, "Oh, chile, I gotta go," and he hung up just like that.

Royal mentally noted the address and swallowed the hard lump of truth that had formed in her throat. She kept pretending to talk to somebody. "Oh, I'm sorry, sir. You were talking so soft and low that I thought you were your wife. Yes, sir . . . Well, I will send you a gift certificate." Royal rolled her eyes for effect, like the man was going on and on, getting on her nerves. "Okay, bye-bye now."

Ascada let out a sigh of relief. "So it was a businessman. I guess I was just overreacting. Hunter loves me, and besides we just got married." She looked at the seven-carat Harry Winston wedding ring on her slim finger.

Royal watched Ascada swoon over the ring. She was glad that Ascada was blindly satisfied for the moment. But if it had been her lover making and receiving two A.M. and three A.M. calls, she would beat ass first and ask questions later.

Ascada was such a weak woman, Royal hoped what she thought was the truth was definitely false.

CHAPTER 18

The cool October breeze felt nice on Emil's face as she sat on the park bench watching her children and Kemoni play.

"Auntie Emil, *TJ* pushed me down." Kemoni held her dirty hands up for Emil to see the evidence.

"Let auntie wipe them off. *TJ*, touch anyone else and we're going home." She smiled at Kemoni, letting her know that she had taken care of the problem.

Why wasn't it that easy to fix grown-up problems? She still couldn't understand how she could have been missing a book of stamps twice in one week. She was just too careful.

It was a blessing to get the job in the first place. By using her married name, she was able to get over on the felony coming up on her record. Her married name saved her credit and reputation. So why was it so hard for her to stay faithful to something that had been so good to her?

Honestly, she only took that last name, because Teo, *TJ*'s father, refused to straighten up and marry her, so the first nice guy she found, she pussy-whipped, sucked him dry, and stuck her finger out and caught the ice.

And now Teo couldn't leave her pussy alone. The real sad part about the situation was, she couldn't stop giving it to him. What he wanted, he got. Even in her and Mekia's bed. Emil was meeting him tonight to slide down that twelve-inch pole. She shivered at the thought.

Lately he'd been talking to her about taking him back and putting Mekia out. She took out the ring that Teo had given her last week. He even promised that he would take care of her and the kids if she left Mekia. "This is so wrong," she said to herself as she pushed some of her auburn bob behind her ear.

"That's beautiful," a New York accent complimented.

Emil jumped and came face to face with Nevada.

"Say hello to the nice lady, Kamerion."

The round-faced little girl with a long ponytail waved, all the while wiggling to get out of her mother's arms to go and play with the other kids. But Nevada needed her as a bargaining tool, so that Emil wouldn't jump on her.

Emil sat back down. "What do you want?"

"To talk, tell you what I know and found out."

Sliding the ring back into her track jacket pocket, she stared at the sandy-haired, blue-eyed, little girl. No doubt she was Spencer's. "Let her go and play with her sisters."

Nevada looked at Emil's balled-up fist and decided against it. "Just hear me out. It won't take long." She squeezed her wiggling daughter close to her bosom.

Emil looked Nevada dead in the eyes. "Spencer sure didn't give a shit about you, because if he did, he would have explained how we get down. And you wouldn't have walked your naïve ass up to me. Especially after the shit you pulled only a week ago."

Nevada looked at the kids playing. "Is she your sister?"

Emil instantly knew that everything this little broad had said in court was a lie. One thing about Spencer—he never, ever denied his kids. He might shit on the mother, but he loved and took care of his kids. "I have a daughter with Spencer too. As well as being best friends with Moses."

"I'm sorry about court," Nevada said in a low tone.

"You definitely are sorry, saying all that hurtful shit to make Moses mad."

Nevada took in a deep breath. "They paid me."

Emil twisted in her seat to face Nevada. "Sweetie, go and play with the other kids." She forcefully pulled the little girl out of her mother's lap.

Kamerion zoomed over to the other kids.

"Bitch, you better start talkin' fast and don't stop 'til it's all said and done. Or I'm gon' bust yo' ass right here in front of all these people."

CHAPTER 19

Nevada sat back on the bench. "I guess I'll start where it all began."

Nevada met Spencer when he came to New York to close a business deal. Her boyfriend Big D was Spencer's connect. One day they both had to move some product fast and she happened to be their mule.

She flew down the next night, and they drove back to Atlanta. On their way back, they were both tired, and she didn't have a license. The only hotel through this little country part of Florida was booked, but Spencer found some willing people to take five hundred dollars for their room.

They took turns showering, and then he innocently asked her to massage his back and bad hip.

She thought, *Why not*. He was a pretty cool dude, and Big D always talked positive about him.

As she massaged his back, he flipped through the clock radio stations, stopping when he heard a Frankie Beverly & Maze tune. Then he asked her, "How did a young, sexy thang like you get hooked up with Big D ugly ass? No offense, but dude is finished."

Nevada giggled. She knew it was true. When they went out in public everyone stared at the beauty and the beast.

"On the real, though, he saved me."

"Saved you? What he do? Swoop down in a cape and save a hoe?"

Nevada slapped him and slid off his body.

"I'm sorry, I'm sorry. My bad for joking. I don't know you like that. Please come back and rub my back."

"I ain't no hoe," Nevada said with an attitude, as she uncomfortably sat back on the tailbone of Spencer's back.

Spencer lifted up so that she could slide her hot pussy back down to the dip of his back. *Control*, he thought. *It's all mind control.* "Okay, finish." He loved to hear ghetto love stories, to see if any of them could compare to his and the love of his Moses.

She told him that when she was seven, she and her parents were moving from Mexico. Her father was an architect, and her mother was a veterinarian. They were moving their respective practices to New York. Her mother loved to travel and sightsee, so they used the move as an excuse to do just that. But her father was extremely tired, and he refused to let the movers get there first and break all of his expensive house models.

He accelerated on the gas when he thought it was the brake, crossed the lane, and hit a tractor-trailer head-on. Nevada was thrown from the car into the uncut grass before the car ignited into flames, killing both her parents, her dog, and her identity.

Every piece of identification, dental records, school records, and old addresses were burned to a crisp by the time the police and fire department got there. They found Nevada unconscious.

Once they got her to the hospital, they determined she was a light-skinned black, female child because of her toasty-brown complexion, full lips, and thick, curly hair. But they were all wrong. She was as white as snow. She had just been in the Mexico sun for a year and tanned very easily. And when New York's Department of Family and Children Services arrived, they also claimed her to be black.

For six months Nevada would not talk, so they put her in an all-black foster home. Her foster mother was taken with the child, nurturing and caring for Nevada like she was her own.

But when she turned fifteen, she began to rebel, running the streets all times of night, and became very disrespectful.

Being fast, she stepped on a few toes, and some girls were about to re-design her face. But Big D saw what was happening and rescued her.

"Damn, you got to be shittin' me?" Spencer asked with sadness in his voice. "How old are you now?" He wanted to make sure she was legal before he took her in his arms and comforted her.

"Eighteen."

"And as he made slow, sweet, sensual love to me, I cried. I cried because I had never felt comfortable enough to tell anyone else in this world that story. Not my foster mom, the social workers, nor Big D." Nevada smiled. "And he had the best dick I had ever had."

Emil gave her a you-better-hurry-up-and-finish-before-I-kick-yo'-ass look.

"Four months later, I found out I was pregnant and I knew that it was Spencer's. And I wanted to keep my baby. But I also knew that Big D would send me home to my mother in a body bag, with my baby on my chest. So I got in touch with Spencer to tell him and see if he wanted to be a couple, to raise the baby."

White folks, Emil thought.

"But he told me that he was in a serious relationship with the woman he planned on marrying and that they had a daughter."

Nevada was hurting as she repeated Spencer's words. She wondered if Emil had felt the same way before.

Emil sat next to Nevada stunned at all of this information. But she hoped Nevada didn't think that she still had feelings for Spencer, because that was so long gone. She loved him as Kaylen's father, but she knew any other kind of love could murder your heart and soul.

Nevada continued, "He told me that he would take care of his child and get me anything I needed. I told him that I had to disappear. So he bought me a condo in Florida and gave me a thousand dollars a week until I had the baby and found a job.

"After I had her and found a decent job at the bank, he faithfully put two thousand dollar a month in my account, and anything else she needed. He would come to Florida every other month and spend a week with Kamerion."

Emil looked at Nevada, waiting for her to confirm the fact that they slept together all those times too.

"He stayed at my house, but we never slept together again, not even to this day. But then the strangest thing happened. As soon as I got the news that my job was transferring me to Atlanta, Spencer stop putting the agreed amount of money in my account. I gave it a few months of calling every day, but to no avail.

"I thought he had been killed or locked up. I thought maybe Moses found out and made him stop sending the money. I let the bad thoughts take over and I filed for child support. My child was crying about her father, and this was the only way I knew I would be able to track him down."

Emil was thoroughly entertained by all this, but she had to get her four kids home, bathed, fed, and bedded so she could get dicked down. "Okay, enough with the sob story. Who in the fuck paid you to fuck with Moses?"

Nevada couldn't remember the lady's name. "She said that she was the judge's assistant. She told me that other women were taking Spencer to child support court. She said all I had to do was say the stuff I did in court, and the judge would make sure I got more than what I was getting a month. But I told her that I made decent money on my job. I only needed the money I was getting, plus the months he'd skipped. I told the lady that I didn't want to cause any trouble. My true intentions were for Kamerion to see her father."

Emil bent over, hugging her knees into her chest. "Ahhh man, the judge, that sneaky sonofabitch. He done went too far this time."

"You know the judge?"

"Personally."

"I'm so sorry for all of this. I wanted to run out the courtroom once I figured out what was going on, but the lady said that if I didn't do as they told me, they would take Kamerion. I wanted to contact Mo but—"

"No, you didn't. You could have done the right thing, but you didn't. So contacting Mo would have and will be murder." Emil looked at her watch and began gathering her things. It was five P.M. and she had to meet Teo at eight.

"Please tell Moses everything I've told you. Here"— Nevada wrote down her home, cell, work numbers, and address—"give this to Moses please."

Emil snatched the paper, grabbed her things, and rushed her kids to the car. She held the piece of paper in her hand, debating whether to give it to Mo and tell her everything, or to let the wind take the number down the street. Mo had been so happy lately with Spencer out of her life. Yet, Emil also knew that Mo missed and loved him and would eventually go back.

But right now she was seeing a new man, and he was like new medicine to the bloodstream, fresh, full of potential, strong, and compatible to the needy body.

Emil stuffed the number in her astray and decided to tell Mo, once she'd given this new guy a chance to come in, and then let her decide.

CHAPTER 20

Even the smell of his green, blue, and silver business card made Mo shiver. She took it out every day just to smell it and envision him. It'd only been three months since they'd met outside the Fulton County Courthouse, but it seemed like an eternity.

They had only been on two quickie lunch dates because of his busy schedule. The first was at the Cheesecake Factory and only lasted twenty minutes before the news station had a breaking story and needed him in front of the camera. The second was long enough for them to get the usual over with. Where you from? Seeing anyone? Kids? And can we continue this on our next date?

But what really pulled her in were the lengthy late-night phone conversations. That's how they explored each other's worlds, and got to know each other. She felt like a teenager again.

Mo surprised herself at how comfortable she had become with him. When he invited her to dinner at his home, she accepted immediately. She couldn't wait to be in his presence again. His cinnamon-colored dimples, sleepy eyes, thick eyelashes, and charming voice, not to mention his wardrobe, was enough to give him anything he wanted from her. But Mo decided to take it slow. She didn't want another dog in her heart.

All in all, Mo was a good person with a bad past and no positive guidance along the way. She thought what Spencer had done by "saving" her was the greatest thing anyone could have done for her. But the more she thought about it . . . he was just another trap. He had a lot of money and some decent sex, but he too neglected her emotional and nurturing needs.

She wasn't the typical dope man's bitch with the nails, hair, expensive jewelry, high-end designer clothes, or slick tongue, and always with ulterior motives. How could these women be happy? They had to share the money with his mama's mortgage, his sister's car note, the brother's bond, his locked-up homeboy, lawyer fees, other women and child support. Not to mention his own selfish wants. So what's left for the main lady? She just wanted to love and be loved.

Mo could never hate Spencer. He'd given her Kemoni. And she did hold some responsibility in how he treated her during their relationship, by staying and allowing it all to happen.

CHAPTER 21

Ding-dong! Ding-dong!
"Coming." Mo walked quickly through her small, stylish apartment. It wasn't the fancy, mini-mansion that she'd shared with Spencer, but it was home now. She looked out the peephole, and her heart skipped a beat. She hadn't seen or spoken to him since that day at the courthouse. Emil had been dropping Kemoni off to him. And he used her bank account to deposit thousands of dollars a month.

To regain her composure, she took a deep breath before opening the door. He looked like LL Cool J's twin, just a shade lighter, with light-colored eyes.

"What's up? Emil suppose to drop the girls off to you at three to go trick or treating."

Spencer looked at his watch. "Well, that gives me one hour and seventeen minutes to plead my case."

Mo backed away from the door and let him in.

Spencer looked around the small, but quaint living room and kitchen. He spotted pictures of Kemoni, Mo's clique, her grandmother, but none of him.

The unusual smell of his brown leather jacket mixed with the smell of weed and liquor were making her wet. She nervously sat on her feet, in the single chair, as he sat on the sofa. *Be strong girl. They always come sniffing back around familiar territory.*

He laughed as he made himself comfortable.

"What's funny?" Mo asked, becoming uncomfortable.

"You, man, you. Why yo' sexy ass go sit way over there like you don't know me? Scared I'm gone beat yo' ass for fuckin' wit' my dick?"

Mo became scared. *I'm so stupid! This nigga came to kill me. I should have known he would come after me for messing with his crown jewels.*

"Don't tense up." Spencer smiled. "I would never intentionally hurt you, and you know that."

Scared to death, Mo nodded her head up and down yes.

Spencer began shaking his head back and forth, punching the palm of his hand. "I know I fucked up real bad this time, Mo. Real bad."

Feeling more assured that he wouldn't hurt her, she began to speak her mind. "Yeah, you did and I—"

"Wait a minute, this is my floor to speak. First of all, I want you to know that Pig's baby is not mine. Look at her, compared to all my other kids."

Mo hit her balled-up fist down on the arm of the chair. "I'm so tired of all y'all niggas thinking somebody gotta look like y'all before you claim 'em. All kids don't look alike, so don't pull that bullshit with me." Feeling sick to her stomach, just thinking about all the women he'd cheated on her with, she wrapped her arms around her petite waist.

"I'll prove that shit!" He clapped his hands together. "And, second, I never told that girl I loved her, nor did I move her down here. I'm just sorry I even got mixed up with any of them."

Spencer scooted to the end of the sofa, sitting his elbows onto his knees, resting his chin into his hands. "Girl, I love you so much. You are my Bonnie, my Lois Lane. I'm jus', I'm jus' tryin' to figure out a way to convince you we can make it work."

He kept his eyes to the floor in case he needed to camouflage the tears he felt welling up inside. "Do you think it's possible for you to forgive me and come home?" He got down on one knee and pulled a baby blue box wrapped with a white bow out of his pocket. "Will you marry me?"

Mo felt the rush to say yes, grab the ring, make love to Spencer, and go home with him, but her mind took over her heart. The lump in her throat was choking her. She had to know. "Is Layla's baby yours?"

Spencer hesitated for a second. He wanted to lie to her, get her back home, and then tell her the answer to her question. But he owed Mo the truth. "Yeah." He rubbed his hands over his head down to his face and sat back on the sofa.

Mo let out a deep sigh and a flood of tears. At that very moment, they both knew it was finally over. They were both silent for a few minutes.

Spencer was crushed, sick, and lonely for Mo, but he loved her enough to digest all the pain and hurt of losing her, to let her go.

He slipped his leather jacket back on and motioned for Mo to stand up and give him some love. They hugged for what seemed like hours.

"Just so you know, sexy, when you left a year and a half ago, that's when I started fuckin' wit' Layla."

Mo thought for a moment back to a year and a half ago when she went to the doctor and they told her that her reproductive organs were damaged by untreated chlamydia and it didn't look possible for her to have any more children. Mo put him out and didn't talk to him for two months.

"So that's who you shacked up with. Always wondered who it was. A fake-ass wannabe me."

"She was something to take up the loneliness. A stupid mistake. The door is always open for you." He began to walk out the door and remembered he had a gift for Mo. "Oh, here, this is for you." He handed her Lyfe's *The Phoenix* CD. "Number twenty-eight please."

"Now?"

"Naw. Wait until you're alone."

Mo slipped on her shoes and walked him out to the car. They were so wrapped up in the conversation that they didn't pay attention to the dusty old gray Ford Taurus sitting two cars over from Spencer's Cayenne truck.

CHAPTER 22

Layla sat behind the wheel of the borrowed Ford Taurus and stared intensely at the way Spencer and Mo playfully held hands and talked. Her anger was boiling over. *That muthafucka over here cuddling up to the same ho who literally burned his dick. The same dick I spent months sucking back to health.* Seething, she banged her head on the steering wheel. Her mouth became wet, and her head begin to swim.

Spencer leaned back on his truck and fumbled with the ring box in his pocket. "So who is this, oh lame, square-ass nigga that's gon' be around Kemoni?"

Mo looked surprised. "You stalkin' me now?" she asked playfully.

"You know I run these streets. They gon' always be loyal to me. They gon' let me know what's going on wit' mine."

Mo hit Spencer in the chest. "I ain't yours no—"

He grabbed her, making her fall into his chest and arms. "You will always be mine, sexy." He took the ring out of his pocket and placed it on her right ring finger. "Whenever I see it on the left hand, I'll know that you are ready."

And with that, they sealed the deal with a last kiss.

The pressure in Layla's head felt like it had popped. The blood seemed to have drained from her body. Her ears went deaf, and the only thing she could see and hear was, *Kill Moses Whyte.*

She jumped out the car like a wild woman and rushed Mo from behind, grabbing her by the ponytail and slamming her head into a burgundy Camry parked next to Spencer's truck. Mo's face hit the car so hard, it chipped her left canine tooth and split her lip in half.

Layla was grunting like a wild animal fighting for its life. Catching Mo off guard, she was getting the best of her. She stomped Mo into the concrete like she was an invasive roach in her favorite dish.

Spencer grabbed Layla's hand and pulled her off Mo. When she snatched away, though, he yelled out in pain. She had deeply cut his wrist with a rusty box cutter, and blood was gushing out of his wrist.

"Hoe, you thought I was gon' let you take what was mine again?" She spat in Mo's face. "You deserve to die." She grabbed Mo's ponytail with her left hand and put her right foot on her back arching her neck into the air.

"Nooooo!" Spencer yelled out. He grabbed her again. This time she had half of Mo's ponytail in her hand.

As they tussled over the box cutter, Mo leaped up bleeding and hurt. But years of anger, mixed with adrenaline running through her veins, took over. She punched Layla in the temple, knocking her off balance. Mo grabbed her around the neck, pressing her thumb into her trachea, struggling to get the blade from her.

Spencer quickly tore his T-shirt and wrapped it around his open wrist and sliced hand.

Mo banged the back of Layla's head into Spencer's driver

window until it burst into pieces. "Eat glass again, bitch."
And as she pressed her head and neck into the jagged pieces
of glass, she brought the razor diagonally across Layla's
face, slicing it open like a toasted hotdog bun.

By this time, Spencer had fallen out because of the
amount of blood loss, and neighbors started to fill the yard
because of the screeching scream Layla let out.

The woman that lived above Mo came out the door,
wrapped in a baby blue, terry cloth robe and matching
slipper with a bat and her cordless phone. "What's going
on out—" She dropped the bat when she saw Layla's open
face and screamed out in horror at all the blood and open
flesh.

Just as the lady began to dial the police, Chuck, one of
Spencer's workers snatched the phone out of her hand and
slammed it into the concrete. (Spencer had managed to
chirp him as he was losing consciousness.) He handed her
a thousand dollars and directed her back into her apartment, and his other partners did the same for the other
four potential witnesses.

Spencer's soldiers put him in the back seat of his
Cayenne.

Since Mo refused to go to the hospital, Chuck carried
her into her apartment. He looked at her blood-covered
face. "Shawty, you gon' be all right? You look like you
need some stitches."

She stretched out on the floor. "I'm straight. This is
more her blood than mine."

"Call me. I'm out."

Mo watched from the window to see him throw Layla
into the black van that they'd pulled up in and disappear
like nothing had happened. Mo held on to her side as she
rushed to the mirror to assess the damage to her face. She
turned on the water and washed the blood off her hands
and face. When she looked back into the mirror, it didn't

look as bad as she thought it would. Her lip was split, but that would heal clean. And her hair was cut up to her lower neck, but that would grow back. The chipped canine tooth didn't take away from her appearance, and she planned on seeing her dentist first thing in the morning.

She checked her body from head to toe, making sure she was intact. She ran a hot bath, poured two bottles of witch hazel in the water to take out the soreness, and grabbed her cell phone.

"Hello," the soothing voice answered.

"Hi, Jovan. Kemoni is si—"

"I'll make some homemade chicken noodle soup, bring the calamine lotion, and a *Class of 3000* video."

This is what I'm talking about. Perfect. Always on time.

"All that sounds wonderful, but I'm going to quarantine us and call you when it's all over."

"Call me, text me, let me know if there's anything you need."

After she cancelled her date, and got out the hot bath, she took two 800 milligram Motrin, called Emil and told her what happened.

"Let's do this bitch, Mo. Leave her stankin' in front of her mama's door."

"I ain't going back to jail for no sorry-ass bitch. It's done. I handled it."

"Awight. If you say so."

"Just keep Kemoni with you this week please."

Mo hung up and fell into a deep sleep.

CHAPTER 23

Thanksgiving Day was planned out to a T. Emil cooked all the food, while Ascada hosted the feast at her home. Since Spencer wanted all his kids for the holiday, they declared November 22, 2006 "The Clique day."

Lately everything was running smoothly in all of the women's lives. Emil's husband Mekia, picked up a part-time job to help make ends meet. Royal was finally going to introduce everyone to her mystery lover. Mo was also bringing her new man, and Joc had finally asked Pepper to marry him, and he was coming to mingle and get to know her "loser friends." And Ascada had put her obsession with Hunter's cheating out of her mind.

But tonight would be the start of a two-week domino effect of bad luck and the test of their friendships and relationships.

"I hope this is enough, fool." Emil took the vegetable casserole out of the oven.

"It should be fine. We don't have the rug rats to feed, and I think you covered the entire menu twice." Ascada laughed as she stuffed a piece of ham and cornbread in her mouth.

"If I didn't know any better, I would say you were pregnant." Emil leaned back on the counter to get a better look. "Those little hips of yours are spreading."

Pepper popped a small block of cheese into her mouth. "Who pregnant?"

"Nobody. I took a home pregnancy test and it was negative. Plus, my period is on."

"So what that mean? Remember Mo bled for four months with Kemoni." Pepper slid a piece of sliced hen into her mouth.

"You keep on eating like that and you gon' look pregnant," Emil said to Pepper.

"Fuck you. My man love it."

"Yeah, for now, 'cause once you pack up that wedding dress he gon' start talking shit." Ascada was feeling her own insecurities about how Hunter had treated her.

"Where's Mekia?" Pepper said, changing the subject.

"He went to the airport to pick up his cousin Koi."

"Where she from?"

"Delaware, out of all places. She suppose to be moving here to get a fresh start. She gon' stay with us for a few months until she get on her feet."

Joc sat stiffly as he drank his third glass of Patrón. Pepper watched him as he continuously hit the end button on his cell phone.

"What time is Royal's black ass gettin' here?" Ascada whined. "I'm hungry."

Hunter was walking around impatiently, like he had somewhere else to be. Ascada walked over to the corner of the room where he'd alienated himself and stood beside him. If not for her mother and his family, she knew that he wouldn't have been there. "Hunter," she said sweetly, lovingly caressing his shoulder, "you all right, honey?"

He noticeably jerked his shoulder away. "Just ready to get this hoax over with."

Ascada's heart was in her throat, but she needed to know. "Do you have another family to be with?"

Hunter looked like a deer caught in headlights. He made sure no one was in earshot. "How dare you question me, Ascada? I'm out here working all day into the wee hours of the morning to give you a million-dollar home, a chauffeur to drive your useless ass around, a maid, and five thousand a month allowance because your dumb ass can't support yourself due to your young stupidity."

His neck was flared like a cobra. Ascada was waiting for him to strike any second.

"And you have the nerve to come at me like that? Bullshit!" He walked over to his parents, leaving her dumbfounded, and scared.

The door bell rang, and Mekia walked in with his cousin Koi behind him. Everyone stared in amazement at what little clothes covered her giant ass. Her long, curly weave, extra thick, fake eyelashes, and overdone makeup made her a sure-fire candidate for prostitute of the year.

"Son, who is that young lady?" Mayor Cambell asked his son. He was whorish and she fit the bill.

Hunter looked on in disgust. "Father, I'm sorry you had to be subjected to this mess."

Mayor Cambell smiled and patted his son on the back. "I wouldn't have missed it for the world. It's good to be in reality after being in front of the camera and fake politicians all day. Find out who the young lady is and introduce us."

"What's up, everybody?" Mekia walked over and kissed Emil. "This is my wife and her other family."

Koi stood shyly, seductively batting her eyes at the men in the room to see who she had the potential to hook. She danced in rap videos for a living. But once she had slept with the majority of the industry and the word spread that she was a stalker, she was blackballed from any video sets.

"Somebody must have misinformed her that we were having a porno movie audition," Emil whispered in Mekia's ear.

"It's a pleasure to meet you all," she said, eyeing Joc and Mayor Cambell.

Pepper picked right up on it. She flashed her ring as she walked by Koi, sitting damn near in Joc's lap. "He already knows me."

Ding-dong! Ding-dong!

"Saved by the bell." Ascada rushed to the door, almost tripping over Koi's glass four-inch heels. She opened the door and closed it back fast.

Her mother asked, "Who is it, Ascada? Royal?"

CHAPTER 24

What in the hell is Royal doing? Ascada thought surely this would drive both Hunter and Joc right out of her and Pepper's lives.

Pepper pushed past Ascada and opened the door. She stared at Royal for what seemed like hours, squeezing the door between her sweaty fingers. *Why is she doing this now? Right after Joc has asked me to marry him. I'm either going to have to let my best friends go or let him go.*

Royal pushed the door open and walked in. "Hello, everyone."

Ascada's mother rushed over to her niece. "Chil', am I glad you are here. We were about to starve. You look nice. Could use a little color, but otherwise, you lookin' good." Ascada's mother was so fake, always ready to bust someone's bubble. "Who is this pretty girl?" She grabbed the young lady's hand. "You should have passed on some of your makeup techniques to Royal."

Mayor Cambell looked at all the fresh young meat in the room. "We are going to have to have more gatherings."

Hunter rolled his eyes at his father's comment. He

couldn't believe his father was truly entertained by the garbage standing in the middle of his living room.

"Who is this lovely girl, Royal?" Ascada's mother asked again. "I've never seen her over to the house."

Just then, Mo and Jovan walked in bearing red velvet and kiwi cakes. Mo winked at Royal. She'd begged her to come out of the closet a long time ago.

"Brooke, this is my family, and everyone this is Brooke . . . my girlfriend." Royal's smooth, dark chocolate skin and crystal-clear colored eyes sparkled as she said her lover's name.

Again, everyone's mouth was left open.

Ascada's mother slung Brooke's hand like it was a diseased rag. She put her drink down and grabbed her coat. "She ain't any family of mine. Dirty selves! And if you had any kind of sense she wouldn't be none of yours either. What kind of good Christian husband like you gon' put up with this mess?" She looked at Hunter for support.

He gulped down his drink and left her to stand on her own.

She walked over to Royal's face. "You know what type of life Ascada has now. Why would you bring this filth in her house? Haven't you burdened her life enough with all your secrets? Since you cleansin' your soul, why don't you tell 'em everything?" She made eye contact with Mo and, with that, walked out the door.

Mekia, being the good guy that he was, walked over to them, smiled, shook Brooke's hand, and hugged Royal. "Hey, what's up?"

"Thanks, Mekia," Royal whispered in his ear.

"What did she mean by that, Royal?" Mo asked.

Royal shrugged her shoulders and pretended that the whole scene didn't take place.

Pepper and Emil walked over like a set of Siamese twins. "Hi, how are you?" they asked Brooke. Then they bumped heads trying to hug Royal at the same time.

Royal squeezed Pepper close to her. "I'm sorry, *P*. I know Joc already think we ain't shit, but she makes me happy."

Hunter looked at Ascada in disgust. Joc looked at the group of women with lust, watching for an opportunity. And Mr. Cambell wanted them for himself. He would definitely be slipping his card to Koi.

After everyone was full off food and liquor, everyone dispersed except The Clique and their significant others. At five o'clock Mo received a threatening phone call on her cell phone. "Stupid ho, yo' life is going to end at six."

Mo walked away from everyone so that they wouldn't hear her phone call. "Who the fuck is this? Woman up."

The angry voice asked, "Oh, you think because you slice somebody face in half that you untouchable?"

"Damn right! Now bring yo' ass back so I can finish the job, this time starting with yo' asshole."

"Oooh no, hoe! You gon' get it in more ways than one." And the voice hung up.

"Let's go, gotdamn it!"

"Joc, why are you acting like this?" Pepper yanked her arm from him. "I thought you were having a good time."

He snatched her arm again, and said through clenched teeth, "Bring your ass on right now!"

Everyone looked in their direction.

"Joc, if you want to go, then go, but I'm not ready to leave."

Joc snatched Pepper by the collar of her silk, ruffle blouse, tearing it as he dragged her to the door.

Mekia held on tight to Emil's waist. "Leave it alone."

Ascada stood scared and silent, by the telephone, just in case she had to call the police.

Royal quickly stepped out of her shoes, but Brooke grabbed her by the hand. "Let them handle their business."

"Look, this is my clique. We ride or die for each other. So unless you part of the solution, then you are part of the problem." She rushed over to Pepper and Joc. "What's the rush, Joc? We have plenty to drink. And if you are ready to go, I can drop Pepper off at home."

"We got plenty to drink at home. And perhaps you've gotten confused. This is my woman, and we are tired."

Mo was a little tipsy and feeling uninhibited. "Ahh, Joc, you scared to leave her in the company of real men?"

Jovan pulled her into the bathroom.

Pepper felt a new sense of fearlessness and snatched away from Joc. "Yo' ass is tired! Real tired!" She threw his jacket at him. "You don't control me. I'm a grown-ass woman. Leave!"

Bam, bam, bam! Ding-dong, ding-dong!

Eyeing Ascada, Hunter went to open the door. "This is probably the bearded lady coming to join this circus in my living room."

CHAPTER 25

Before Hunter could open the door, a statuesque, curly-haired brunette dressed in all white with a waist-length mink pushed her way into the house. "Where the fuck is my husband?"

Coming out of the bathroom, Mo said with an attitude, "Honey, who the fuck is your husband?" She looked accusingly at Jovan, and he shrugged his arms and shook his head no.

Ascada held on to her heart. She just knew it. She told Royal. She looked at Hunter, and he lowered his bottom lip and threw his hands in the air to say not him.

The brunette walked over to Joc and slapped the shit out of him. "You fuckin' bastard."

He retaliated and knocked her to the floor. "Bitch, if you ever touch me like that again, your body will be floating up the river." He grabbed Pepper by the arm, attempting to pull her to the door.

The lady laying on the floor began crying, not from the blow she took from Joc's hand, but from what he was holding with his other. Pepper. He'd told her several times that he'd found the love of his life and that she was black and beautiful, a blow to her Italian self-esteem.

"Please, Joc . . . I love you," she said, grabbing him around the leg. And instead of looking like the beautiful porcelain doll that barged her way into the door and demanded her husband, she now looked like a wimpy puppy. "You don't need this black bitch—"

Mo walked up on the lady. "Umm, honey, get cho ass up outta here before we black bitches show you what we made of."

Pepper was speechless. She couldn't say anything. At this point she knew Joc wanted her, had blatantly chosen her, but that didn't change the fact that he was still married.

Emil wiggled away from Mekia and stood next to Mo. "Joc's wife," she said with emphasis so that Pepper would take notice, "get yo' pitiful ass up off this floor and leave."

Joc continued to pull Pepper by her arm, dragging the lady in white by his leg out the front door. Joc's wife held on tight as he dragged her to the hallway.

Emil, Mo, and Royal were trying to free his hands off Pepper.

"This black bitch isn't going to stay with you. She's a whore! They'll never accept her. I was your ticket in, and I'll be your ticket out." She gathered all the saliva in her throat and mouth and spat on Pepper's legs and shoe.

Pepper pushed Joc, and he fell, tripping over his wife. Pepper began to stomp her in the face.

Ascada screamed and dialed the police. Hunter grabbed his coat and left.

Mekia grabbed Emil by the waist and took her back into the apartment before she could deliver her second blow to the now lady in red, blood coming from her nose, face, and mouth.

Jovan grabbed Mo, as Brooke pulled Royal and she

grabbed Pepper back into the penthouse, locking the door, leaving Joc and his wife in the hallway.

He rammed her with all his might and brought his heavy fist into her stomach, knocking the fight out of her. As she moaned and rolled around on the floor he told her, "You better pray this mink floats." He snatched her by the hair and dragged her to the elevator kicking and screaming.

Pepper placed her hands and face on the door, crying profusely, letting her feet slide from beneath her.

Ascada ran into her bedroom, laid across her bed, and cried like a baby. They had ruined her life once again. Hunter was never going to come back after this.

Mo, Emil, and Royal crawled over to Pepper on their knees and hugged each other.

The first domino had fallen.

CHAPTER 26

Royal released the last puff of smoke from the much-needed blunt as she leaned against the kitchen counter.

Brooke took the roach from her and threw it in the ashtray. She tongue-kissed Royal passionately as she removed her blouse. "Let me suck on that sweet pussy." Brooke licked and sucked Royal's swollen breast. She held one in each hand and pushed the nipples together, devouring them, licking them slow at first, arousing them, then flicking her tongue fast against their hardness and driving Royal wild.

As Brooke held one of Royal's breasts in her mouth, she slid her other hand under her skirt, running her hand over Royal's thick, dark chocolate thighs. She was truly in love with Royal. This was just one of Brooke's countless lesbian relationships, but Royal's first. She knew that Royal wasn't truly gay, just going through an I-hate-men phase. But after all the head and bumping pussy they did, she was hoping Royal would be convinced to stay.

Brooke slid Royal's panties down and helped her sit and

lean back on the countertop. She pushed Royal's legs back, placing her feet on the counter as anchors. Then she slid her arms underneath both sides of Royal's thick legs, grabbing a handful of soft, full hips and ass, pulling her hot, wet pussy to her mouth.

"Can I smell this good pussy?" Brooke teased.

"Yes."

Brooke teased her manicured mound, blowing hot air and lightly tapping her clit with the tip of her nose. When Royal inched up on the counter, Brooke aggressively grabbed her pussy back to her face. "Can I taste you, baby?"

"Yes." Royal panted as she anticipated Brooke's juicy lips on her throbbing pussy.

She kissed it with pressure two times. Then she licked the entire circumference of her valley as she pulled Royal's ass closer, Royal's big ass hanging halfway off the counter as Brooke tongue-kissed the inside of her pink pussy.

"Ummm, Brooke, yessssssss . . . yessssssss!" Royal slung her head back, knocking it into the cabinet, the pain intensifying the heat that she was feeling between her thighs.

Brooke munched on her clit with only her lips, lightly darting her tongue to medium rhythm. "Damn! This pussy sweet."

Royal grabbed a handful of her hair and pushed her deep into her cup of overflowing juices. "Eat this pussy. Eat it up. Uhhhh!"

Brooke slurped all of Royal's juices up then gently shook her face back and forth, her chin tapping the palms of her rotund ass.

"Ahhhh, ahhh, ooooh, I'm 'bout . . . sssss . . . to cum! Damn!"

"Not yet," Brooke whispered. She kissed her sweet pussy and let her down off the counter. Then she led her to the living room floor, where they both became fully naked.

Royal lay out on the soft black shag rug as Brooke lit several scented candles.

Brooke turned on the stereo, and Tweet began to play.

Royal lay back as Brooke, licking from her toes up to her vagina, took control.

As Royal sat up, Brook slid her left leg under Royal's right leg, and her right leg over her left. She then scooted up until their pussies were kissing and rolled her hips around, mushing her pussy into Royal's, their wet caves leading each other into ecstasy.

Brooke grabbed her own two breasts and pushed them into her mouth, sucking hard, as her hips picked up speed. As she worked Royal, she yelled out, "Gotdamn, Royal, this pussy is the best!"

Brooke reached her hand between their legs and brought her wet fingers to Royal's mouth. When Royal refused, as she usually did, she licked them herself, enjoying the smell and taste of her lover. "You wanna cum, Royal?"

"Yes . . . ummm, yes!" she answered faintly, taken over by the pleasure her body was receiving.

Brooke lifted up on her left hand and slightly twisted her body as she quickly dipped up and down, back and forth into Royal's slippery, wet, fat pussy.

Royal grabbed onto Brooke as Brooke slammed her ass into Royal. "I'm comin'!"

Brooke twisted her body, throwing her right leg over Royal's head, and began winding and grinding.

Royal screamed out in satisfaction, "Yessss . . . uhhhh . . . fuck me . . . Ooooh shitttddddd!"

Brooke rapidly jiggled her soft, wet ass, plunging into Royal, until she began to jerk. Seeing her cum and feeling that juicy, wet pussy, and thick ass beneath her made her own body convulse.

CHAPTER 27

Ring, ring, ring!
Mo raised up on her elbows and peered at the clock sitting on the nightstand. It read three-eighteen. She looked over at Jovan sleeping peacefully. Was this deja vu? Her mind began to race out of control. She was scared to look at her cell phone.

Ring, ring, ring!
Now Jovan's house phone was ringing. This was definitely happening again. Mo jumped out of the bed and ran to the window to see what woman was sitting outside waiting for her. She was going crazy.

"What? How the hell did that happen?" she heard Jovan say into the phone. "We're on the way."

Jovan jumped up and grabbed his pants. "Moses, put on your clothes."

She knew this shit was too good to be true. As she angrily threw on her clothes she said, "I told you everything that I've been through and let you in my heart and life. And now you doin' the same shit he did. I'm so fuckin' stupid."

Jovan didn't now how to tell Mo what was happening. He felt sorry for her with all the drama, lies, disappointment, hurt and Spencer's bullshit coming at her unmercifully. He walked over to her and tried to hold her by the waist. "Bay, I—"

"Bay, hell! I'm tired of this shit! I think Royal got the right idea."

How could she think that he wanted another woman? She consumed his every thought. He wanted to take care of her and Kemoni, protect and love her. Maybe in his rough past he would have fucked her over, but she was his future.

Not knowing any other way to say what he had to say, he blurted, "Spencer was busted in the biggest drug bust in Georgia."

Mo held her stomach. "Where's my baby, Jovan?" She walked over to him and looked up into his eyes. "He had drugs in the house with all his kids there? Naw, I don't buy that. He would never, ever put those girls' lives at risk like that."

Jovan sat Mo down on the bed. "That's why Meno, my camera man, my best friend called me. He said it was a weird bust because no drugs were in the house, but they took him anyway. They collected all the dope and money from other locations and then went to the house and arrested him and his mother at six o'clock on Thanksgiving Day." He shook his head. "Something isn't right."

Mo thought back to the phone call. The caller said six o'clock. Somebody had set them up. She was frantic. "Where's Kemoni and Kaylen?"

"Baby, calm down."

"Where's my gotdamn child?" she screamed.

"DFACS."

CHAPTER 28

Four days later, on a windy, raining Monday morning, Mo and Emil stood first in line at the Fulton County Jail to see Spencer.

They spent their entire Friday, the day after Thanksgiving Day, calling and riding back and forth from the jail and DFACS, trying to get their children back.

With teary, bloodshot eyes Emil looked helplessly at Mo. "I'm gon' fuck Ascada up if she don't get her scary ass over to Hunter's office and ask him to make a phone call to the city."

Mo folded her arms, leaned against the wall, and let out a loud, lengthy sigh. "I'm tired. I'm so tired of going through stuff because of Spencer. I'm not even with him no more and he's still causing me pain."

"Visitors to see Spencer Mack, have your ID out and remove all rings—ear, tongue, eyebrows—and belts."

Spencer was already sitting in the seat behind the glass with a cold stare. He'd only been in jail for four days, but the cell that he lay his head in had his name on it for the last four months.

Half the jail dapped him when he arrived, letting him know they had his back. He was a well-respected man on the streets, and it carried over to jail as well. But something was sheisty, and he would definitely not trust anyone and always watch his back. His boy Kane was on his same block, and one of his soldiers was going to get himself a small charge to be in with Spencer. So that put him at ease.

How could this bullshit have happened? He had everything in order and under control. Everything, but the women in his life.

Emil picked up the phone first. "I never trusted your low-down ass with nothing but Kaylen. How could you let this happen?"

He looked her dead in the eyes. "Somebody set me up."

"What do you mean? Who?"

He leaned back in his chair. "I don't know. Ever since court"—he looked at Mo—"shit ain't been right."

Mo snatched the phone from Emil. "Bitch, I know you ain't accusing me of setting you up."

"You layin' up with police, ain't you?"

At first she didn't understand what he meant by the comment. Then when she did, she said, "Nigga, he ain't the damn police. Jovan is a news reporter. And he the one tryin' to help yo' ass by calling in favors to find out why the Feds did this."

Spencer looked at Mo's right hand, and the seven-carat diamond ring. He already knew she would never do anything like that to him, but he had to cover his back. "Naw, baby. I'm just . . . just messed up right now. And somebody who knew me well set me up and took my seeds away."

Emil and Mo sat in the chair together, sharing the phone between their ears. Mo said, "Answer me this—why was Kaja not there?"

"Because Pig said that if I didn't take them both that I couldn't take Kaja. And that ain't my baby, Mo."

"I know," they said in unison.

Emil told him, "So she got pissed, and you know how vengeful she is."

"Nope. Pig didn't know all my spots and where I kept my money."

Mo asked, "What about Chuck? Your runners? Connects?"

"Naw, they had just as much to lose, if not more." Spencer ran his hand over his head. "I'm fucked up. I never thought I would say that. I thought money could take care of everything, but I guess somebody feelings got caught up. What did they say about my girls?"

"Ascada is on her way to see Hunter. He should be able to do something. But the DFACS office said they were ordered by the court not to talk to us." Mo sighed heavily and leaned back in the chair. "It's going to be fifty thousand dollars apiece to retain Humphries, and that's a deal."

"It's going to be two hundred fifty thousand dollars for my case. But he's willing to work with us. I put about twenty-five thousand in an account under Kemoni name. Get it out and use it to pay bills and give him half. I'll take care of myself."

Emil tried to be strong and choke back tears, but after a few minutes of thinking about the possibly of losing Kaylen again, she broke down. "I-I can't do this again." She wiped the spit drooling down the corner of her mouth. "I lost her once before. I can't do it again."

Spencer knew what he had to do. He was going to go against every code of the game, but his kids were more important than honor at this point. "Hey, I got an idea. But y'all are going to have to get some people involved that you don't get along with to get it done. My mama is outside."

"What is it, Spencer? What—"

"I can't discuss nothing on this phone. Go get the stuff from my mama."

After retrieving the instructions from Spencer's mother, Emil and Mo hugged each other.

CHAPTER 29

Emil pulled into her driveway and leaned her head on the steering wheel. She used to wear a smile every time she pulled into her subdivision, but now it seemed like she'd love to be anywhere else but there. Her daughter was gone, the yard was unkempt, and the bills had already doubled since she'd lost her job. And Mekia hurt his back at work. And now that his cousin Koi lay her big, greedy ass around talking on the phone all day, going in and out of the refrigerator, keeping curling irons plugged up, watching endless TV, it was costing them dearly. It's funny how all those things become meaningful when money is a problem.

Emil reluctantly walked through the door, turning off lights in every room, cutting her eyes at Koi, who was lying on the couch, her ass half-exposed, eating chips and watching *All My Children*.

Koi shook the half eaten bag of chips in the air. "We need some more chips and Juicy Juice."

Emil slammed the bill drawer. "We need a damn job!" She walked out of the kitchen and stood in front of Koi, blocking the TV. "Then you could buy your own damn chips"—she snatched the half-eaten bag out of Koi's hand—"and juice, instead of eating up all my kids' stuff."

Koi's spaced-out ass still lay on the sofa, unaffected by what Emil was fussing about. She smirked. "Well, I figured since one of 'em was gone, I might as well take up the slack."

Just as Emil was about to put a foot up Koi's ass, the door bell rang.

Koi jumped up to answer the door. "Saved by the bell," she said, bouncing and jiggling to the door.

Royal, Mo, and Pepper walked in.

"Why don't you put some clothes on that moose you call an ass." Royal gave Koi a look of disgust.

"I thought you'd like all this ass in your face."

"Okay, okay, battle of the big asses." Mo held her hands up in front of both of them. "We have some serious business to take care of."

Since Koi didn't have a job or any money coming in, and she was the extra hand they needed, Emil offered a place on their team.

Pepper was wrapped up in a big black bubble coat, tennis shoes, and a sad face. She sank down in the round, fluffy chair and waited to hear all the wild survival plans.

Royal poured herself a class of cranberry juice and made Pepper some hot, lavender tea. "What time is Mekia coming back from therapy?"

Emil looked at her watch. "Ahmm, we got at least two hours. But we have four more people coming."

"Four more people? This shaker-booty ho is one too many," Royal said seriously.

"Pussy lips, you sho got a lot to say about me. I told you Em, she wants this hot ass." Koi slapped her monster ass.

"Bitch, you wish." Royal rolled her eyes and walked

over to Pepper. "Take that damn hot-ass jacket off and drink this lavender tea.

Pepper did as she was told then sank back into the well-cushioned oversized chair.

Ding-∂ong, ∂ing-∂ong!

Nevada walked in slowly, bracing herself for a tongue-lashing, possibly brutality, but Emil promised she would handle everything.

Mo jumped up from the sofa. "What the fuck is she doing here?"

"Wait, wait, wait a minute, Mo." Emil stood in front of Nevada. "Her daughter was taken too, and she don't have the money to get the lawyer either. And we need her. Think about Kemoni."

"Fuck that! Who else gon' walk through that door, Layla?"

Emil looked away.

Hurt and betrayal swelled up inside of Mo like a sickness. "Are you fuckin' kiddin' me? You must want blood-shed in dis muthafucka today!" Mo grabbed her coat and purse and headed out the door.

"No." Pepper stood in front of the door. "We need you. Kemoni and Kaylen need you. These other girls want their children too. Fuck Layla."

The doorbell rang twice more, revealing Pig and Ascada, but no Layla. All the women sat around the coffee table with intense looks on their faces as Mo and Emil explained the plan to get their children back and set all of them financially straight for the rest of their lives.

CHAPTER 30

Layla held her head in her hand as the blonde, blue-eyed woman tried to explain that she and Judge Cantrell did everything possible to release Spencer, but were unsuccessful.

"But you told me that once the kids were processed into DFACS that y'all would drop the charges on him." Her knees were bouncing uncontrollably.

"Layla," the soft-spoken blonde woman said, "you are better off without him. We gave you your child back, paid for plastic surgery. Plus, we gave you twenty-five thousand dollars."

"I didn't want him to be convicted. You said that he would only go for a couple of days, long enough to convict Moses of slashing my face. I didn't even know that y'all would do this with all the kids there." Layla began to cry. "I didn't want all this to happen. I just wanted Moses to get hers."

"Look," the blonde woman said in a harsh, nasty tone, grabbing her purse and adjusting her suit jacket, "that bastard got what he deserved, and the little bitch will too. But if you blow this by telling Spencer any of this, he'll never get out, and your child will join her sisters in DFACS custody."

Layla followed her to the door. "I'll go to the police and tell them—"

Gabby swiftly turned around. "Ungrateful bitch, I am the police." Gabby flashed her badge. "Like I said, fuck with me and you will get fucked."

With that, Gabby walked out the door and called Cantrell. "Baby, it's done," she said. "All of them will come tumbling down."

Cantrell sat at his home dialysis machine with a big, satisfied grin on his face. *Those jungle whores will pay for all the damage they've done to my career and body.*

Inside the house, Layla picked up her beautiful daughter. She kissed Kendall on her forehead. "I'm sorry, baby girl, for all the mess mommy has caused in your little life. I got to find a way to get your daddy out of jail. He doesn't deserve to be there."

When the blonde woman first came to see Layla in the hospital, after her face slashing, she'd asked her who did that to her, but Layla wouldn't tell her that Mo was the one who'd cut her.

Spencer had begged her not to go to the police, and eventually persuaded her that if she had not brought the knife and tried to stab Mo, none of this would have happened. But after a couple of weeks Spencer told Layla that he still loved Mo and wanted to marry her and raise his kids as a family.

Enraged, Layla found the card with the woman's name on it and called her. She figured if she got Spencer locked up, then he wouldn't know that Mo was getting arrested and couldn't post bail for her. With her already having a felony, she would be gone for a long time. But now, looking at the big picture, it was all coming back to slap her in the face again.

CHAPTER 31

One week after Thanksgiving, Spencer being locked up, DFACS taking the kids, Pepper leaving Joc, the court ruling Royal to be a fraud, Ascada still hadn't shared the same bed with her husband. He would either sleep on the sofa or at his office.

When the kids were first taken, she asked Hunter to help Emil and Mo, and his response was, "They are better off in there. I'm not putting my name on the line for the likes of them."

For the past week, she wasn't able to get in contact with him at all. She promised Emil and Mo that she would ask him one last time and try to convince him in exchange for their friendship.

Ascada loved the lunch dates in Paris then flying back to New York for the night life. She was the first to admit that Hunter was pushed on her by her mother and his. They looked good together, but nobody cared if they liked each other, let alone loved one another. But the benefits outweighed the faint feelings she had for him.

Hunter was a perfectionist. Neat, organized, well-manicured, and a workaholic. Ascada, on the other hand, was a junkie, lost, irresponsible, and only cared that the price tag on her clothes was at least three digits.

As the driver pulled the car around the court, Ascada looked at the address Royal wrote on the paper and then back at the pale green, trimmed-in-brown dollhouse.

Royal came to the house earlier that morning and said, "Hunter called me today and said he had a surprise for you." She handed her the paper with the address on it and a key. "He said come to this address at nine o'clock. Don't knock or ring the bell. Use the key and go on in."

Ascada stepped out of the car, adjusted her red Cavalli dress, and checked her overdone makeup.

"Mrs., do you want me to wait, or shall I come back when you call?"

"Sherman, you can go home and get some sleep for the both of us." She winked at her driver and tipped him a fifty.

"You sure do look and smell like an angel, ma'am."

She smiled at her driver and walked like a sex kitten to the door.

Pepper leaned over the passenger seat. "I can't believe you lettin' that girl go in that house and get her feelings hurt."

"She wouldn't have believed me if I would have just told her," Royal explained.

"All I got to say is, I hope you already got her naive ass a bed on the thirteenth floor." Emil restlessly adjusted herself in the front passenger seat. " 'Cause she gon' need it after this."

"I just want her to hurry up and get in there so she can make him help us get our girls back." Mo breathed on the cold window, keeping her eye on Ascada as she entered the house. "You sure the cameras are in the right room?"

"I put one in every room. Even the bathroom," Royal told her.

Erotic music and flickering candlelight were coming from around the corner of the foyer. Ascada danced her petite body around in a circle, overcome with excitement that Hunter had forgiven her and was ready to continue their marriage. She placed her Gucci pouch and coat on the French lowboy as she took one last look in the mirror at her hair, makeup, and dress.

Then she walked into the sunken den and saw Hunter on his knees, his back toward Ascada. It was dark in the room, and the low-burning candles illuminated only the entrance to the room. She tried to adjust her eyes and call his name over the loud music, but to no avail. She sashayed over to him but was stopped in her tracks. She strained to see through the darkness and knew what she was seeing must have been a mistake.

Ascada watched Hunter's head move up and down rapidly in between some woman's thighs. Her eyes darted around the room, looking for a light switch. She began to severely itch because of her nervousness. She held on to her stomach for support. She wanted to throw up on them. Not wanting it to be true, she was too scared to just run up on them.

Ascada knew he was cheating. She'd asked him. Why couldn't he just tell her the truth? They could have worked through it. She leaned against a wall and felt a poke in her back, a light switch. She held her breath before she flicked the light on, hoping her eyes were playing tricks on her. But they weren't.

She pushed him in the back. "What the hell are you doing?"

When Hunter rose up and let go of the dick in his mouth, Ascada stumbled sideways, almost falling over.

The sight of the man in the chair, his legs straddled like a woman's, was like being in the twilight zone. She rushed over the stereo system and kicked it in, not realizing that she'd kicked over two small candles.

The young, handsome man with a voice more sensual and feminine than Ascada's got off the chair. "Hunter, what the fuck is going on here? I don't know what kind of kinky shit you thought was going down, but I do not do fish."

Hunter spun around on his knees and came face to face with Ascada. "Ascada, what . . . when . . . how did you find me?" He jumped to his feet, in shock, his whole body shaking from embarrassment. Maybe he could hit her over the head with something, kill her, and tell the police he thought it was a burglar.

"You scandalous, gay, sick bastard. How could you?"

Hunter was fiercely pacing back and forth, concerned with what his father was going to say. *He's going to disown me. I'll lose my inheritance, my position on the counsel, my reputation, all because of this bitch!*

"And you were so disgusted with my cousin, saying all that mean, nasty stuff about Royal, and here you are doing the same disgusting thing." Ascada wiped her wet face. "And you're married to me." Her stomach was doing flips, the vomit lingering in her throat.

Ascada sat down in the same wet seat Hunter and his lover had just fornicated on.

"You? You? You pitiful, needy cunt, what about you? You are a worthless piece of body and soul, the perfect front for my parents."

Hunter walked up so close to Ascada's face, she could smell Eric's dick on his breath.

"You made me sick to my stomach every time I fucked your skinny, stankin' ass." He laughed to himself. "You should have gave that lil' funky pussy to someone who wanted it. Like the butch at Walsh."

Ascada pushed him away and jumped out of the chair. "What's the difference between fuckin' *it* in the ass and fuckin' me in the ass?"

"Unh-uh, unh-uh. I know this fish ain't callin' me no *it*." Eric pushed past Hunter. "Bitch, I'm more woman than you'll ever be. Must be, 'cause I took yo' man." He rolled his neck and circle-snapped his fingers in Ascada's face.

Ascada's stomach was trying to tell her something but the he-she in front of her was holding her attention. Every time she tried to swallow more of the contents of her stomach gushed into her mouth.

"Honey, g'on and pick up your 'tinker bell' shit." Eric began walking around Ascada in a circle, looking her up and down in disgust. "And move on to somebody that gives"—he stuck his neck out and pushed his face into hers—"a fat fuck!"

"Ughhhhhhhhhhh." Ascada violently hurled into Eric's face.

"Bitch!"

And in an instant, a fireball erupted behind the etched wood entertainment cabinet.

"Oh shit!" Hunter screamed out. He ran over to the huge flames, which had now spread to the curtains. "Take off your shirt, baby, and try to fan—I mean smother the flames."

Ascada looked down at her red dress and then over to Eric, who immediately did what her husband told him to.

"Look at what this bitch done did to my palace," Eric cried as he hopelessly, and girlishly, fanned his shirt into the flames.

Ascada walked dazed and lifeless through the foyer. All those dates, all those long talks, kisses and hugs, all the secrets she shared. And now in one night she'd lost her marriage and was being put out by a flaming faggot and her down-low husband.

Not to mention, when the police arrived, they would tell that she started the fire and would be going to jail for a long time because of her prior felony.

When her feet hit the pavement, her knees gave out, and she hit the ground, falling unconscious.

The clique came like thieves in the night, swooped her up, and took her home.

CHAPTER 32

Mo, Emil, Royal and her lover, Pepper, Mekia's cousin Koi, Nevada, and Pig sat in Mo's small living room on December third discussing the final details of their survival plan.

Emil nervously shook her knees and bit her nails. "That sorry bitch better get up outta that bed and make a deal with Hunter so my baby can come home."

"What you want her to do, Emil?" Royal asked. "She just walked in on her husband giving another nigga a blowjob."

"And?"

"And he put her out. She broke as we are now, and you know Ascada is spoiled and scary." Royal took up for her cousin, once again, feeling responsible for messing up her life.

"She's our so-called friend, so she should be just as hell-bent on getting our girls back too!" Emil said.

"She better suck it up and get over it. We got work to do, and we need her," Pepper said, annoyed by Ascada's weakness.

"We gave your ass time to go through mourning when Joc's wife busted up in your life."

"Hoes with no kids make me sick, always trying to have a say-so. Royal, you don't have a child invested in this, so I wouldn't expect you to understand," Emil told her.

Royal wanted to yell at the top of her lungs, "I do! I do understand! I'm invested in this. My child needs money too. His father is locked up too."

"Okay, okay, y'all, let's get back to the matter at hand." Mo looked intensely at Royal. "We'll give her a little time, but Ascada will go after Hunter again and use the fact that he is gay to persuade him to help get our kids back. And since the video tapes were destroyed in the fire, we have no proof."

Mo placed all the self-made packets on the table. Each brown envelope was labeled by states—New York, Philadelphia, Florida, North Carolina, Tennessee, Denver, and Georgia. And in each state-labeled envelope was the exact city, names, addresses, hangouts, habits, the kind of women preferred, and the amount of money and dope of the king-pins and connects that Spencer dealt with.

Mo took the Denver packet for her and Emil. She gave the Tennessee and Georgia packet to Pepper and Koi. The Philadelphia packet went to Royal and Brooke. New York and North Carolina went to Nevada, while Florida went to Pig and Nevada.

"Why do I have three?" Nevada asked, upset.

" 'Cause I thought hoes liked to work," Mo answered, daring Nevada to jump bad.

Pepper didn't want or have time for the catfights. She had her own mouth to feed, and a demo to finish, which would help her get on her feet. And this baby mama drama wasn't going to stand in her way. "Both y'all hoes sit down and calm ya nerves. We all need this money, and so does Spencer in order to get out of jail. Let's stay focused.

"Nevada, I'll take another, if they like brown sugar."
Pepper popped her right hip into the air, trying to lighten
the mood.

Nevada fought back tears. "I can't do New York in any
kind of way." She slid the packet back across the glass and
chrome table.

Emil quickly interjected because she knew her nosy-ass
friends would ask why, and naïve Nevada would tell them
her sob story and Mo would think that she betrayed her.
She meant to tell Mo about Nevada and Spencer, but she
just wanted Mo to experience real love and a real man for
once in her life.

"I know we decided that I wouldn't do any jobs, just in
case sex was involved, because I'm married. But if I have
to, I will. I want my child back."

"Naw, Ascada is gon' take up the slack. It said that he
likes very petite, high-class, black women or white
women. So, Ascada has to do it. He has one of the largest
amounts here." Mo looked into Royal's eyes.

"Why ain't Layla scarface ass in here helpin'?" Pig asked,
high and confused. "We gon' jus' give her the money to get
her chil' back?"

Mo looked at Pepper, Royal, and Emil, and they all
knew at that very moment that Layla had set this whole
thing. They thought she was just being a bitch and didn't
come because of Mo.

"Everybody read and read. Study these packets. Your
attention and focus determines how well we pull this off.
Our faith and trust in each other is how we will survive
this." Mo ran both her hands over her forehead and hair
all the way down to her neck. "And, Pig, please take that
blue weave out of your hair. They like 'em slum in Miami,
but not gutter."

Pig popped her gum and lips loudly as she ran her
hands over her two-hour hair. She thought it was the

bomb. *These hoes think they the shit. I know I'm the shit! My hair ain't never stopped me from getting Mo's man and any other man I wanted. They got this we shit fucked up. I'm working for me.*

"And, Pepper, the muthafucka in Columbus is said to be fine as hell, so stay focused and don't get caught up. I know you vulnerable right now, but this is business. Even the sex."

"Bitch, you don't have to worry about me. I'm on my toes. Worry 'bout yaself." Pepper walked to the bathroom. "You don't get caught up with that white boy in Denver. You might get in touch wit' yo' roots."

"Okay," Mo said, ignoring the hurtful comment, "we'll all go to New York. Nevada, you can stay in the hotel. But Ascada is a fuck-up, and we all need to be on stand-by." Mo sucked in a mouthful of breath. She needed Nevada, but didn't want to need her. "And you know this area better than anybody, so you have to be there. Any questions?"

All the women in the room shook their heads no. In their minds they were already planning their victims' demise.

Mo, Emil, Pepper, and Koi jumped into the rented Ford Taurus and headed to Layla's house.

CHAPTER 33

Layla took the last envelope from the blonde woman and closed the door. She had talked the lady into giving her an extra fifty thousand dollars and a one-way ticket for her and the baby to New York. Layla was a hustler by nature, and she knew how to survive.

When she found out she was pregnant, she hoped Spencer would leave Mo for her, but she didn't bank on it. She found a baller from New York, kicked it with him for a month, and then told him she was pregnant with his child. If it worked out with Spencer, the NY baller would never hear from her again, but everything fell apart.

Ring, ring, ring!

"Hello," Layla answered as she packed her suitcases.

"I tried to love you, but you didn't love yourself. Only the thought of beating Moses at any cost consumed you. I was a conquest for you."

"You let that bitch slice my face in half, Spencer!"

"You brought the knife, Layla. You lost control, and now you want to blame someone else. You were going to cut her face."

Layla's tears came quick and hard. "How could you ask her to marry—"

Spencer's heart softened at the thought of Mo. "I love her. She's my everything."

Layla pinched the baby so she would cry into the phone. "Oh, so you love that bitch more than our baby? Fuck you!"

"Naw, baby girl, you fucked. Tell me something, Layla, how you get Kayla back, while my other daughters lay in foreign beds, being fed by strange hands? And she laying in your arms crying?"

Layla knew Spencer suspected it was her, but she held on to her innocence. "My mama paid for a lawyer, since you didn't leave us no money. What kind of big-time dope man get knocked and don't have any money saved?"

"Bitch, you are dead!" Spencer squeezed the phone, sucking spit through his teeth.

" 'Cause yo' baby mamas couldn't get up they dough, you gon' have me fucked up?" Layla asked, her voice shaky.

"You set all of this in motion. I should've known that you would be the rat, scum, ho to set me up. I hope you know that you are dead, dead!"

"Stop it! You love her—"

"Take my seed to my mother's. I don't want her to get hurt when they leave yo' ass stankin'."

She began to cry profusely. "Please, Spencer, I'm sorry. I'm sorry. I was mad. They paid me, and I needed . . ." She realized that Spencer had hung up.

Spencer sat in his cell reminiscing about his first week being locked up. How depressed he was, thinking about his kids being taken away from their mothers and safe beds and given to strangers because of his stupidity. How did all of this happen?

Three days before Thanksgiving, he and Layla were in a heavy, heated argument.

"So you not gon' put a hit out on that hoe?"

"For what, Layla? You started a fight and lost."

Layla ran her hand down the long bandage on her face. "You think I'm ugly now, don't you?"

"Your looks have nothing to do with why you're ugly." Spencer looked at her with disappointment.

"Do you want me to leave?" she asked, hoping this was just one of his bitchy moods.

"I never asked you to come. At my weakest point you took it upon yourself to move in. I told you Mo was coming home."

Layla picked up a glass vase and threw it at Spencer's head.

He didn't move one bit. He held up his bandaged wrist. "You've already tried to kill me. With Mo not here, I'm already dead."

She took the baby, some money he had stashed, and left in a rage. Revenge was on her mind the minute he asked Mo to marry him.

On Thanksgiving Day, as Spencer watched his daughters play, he thought about his son King. And how he should have been hard enough, tough enough to man up and claim his son to Mo, no matter how much he didn't want to hurt her any more. He'd missed King's first word, laying his tiny body on his chest, hugging him, and telling him, "Daddy is here," and "I love you."

I failed my lil' man. I was supposed to be his protector, teach him how to be a man, and discipline him when he was wrong. I've left him out in the world to battle for himself. I didn't mean for all of this to happen or for my life to turn out like this. In and out, make the money, and don't let it make you. But I let it take control, along with the power and the pussy.

On the days he had his girls, everyone in the streets

knew not to call, come by, or text him because he would not answer. He was in the bathroom when he heard the doorbell.

His oldest, Kaylen, answered the door.

"Where's your daddy, honey?" the white, bearded man with shades asked.

She put her hand on her hip. "Who wanna know 'bout my daddy?"

The other girls joined their leader at the door.

The bearded man with the shades laughed. He stepped closer to the door, gently pushing it with his shoulder, scanning the room for any adult bodies. "I'm a friend of your father's, and I need to see him."

"Well, my daddy don't have company when we here. All his attention and time is on us. We the only ladies in his life." Kaylen saw several men and women moving closer to the house. And the white, bearded man began pushing harder on the door, scaring her. "Daddyyy!"

Spencer was in the middle of a much-needed bowel movement, after taking all the pain medication and antibiotics for his slit wrist. He faintly heard Kaylen's scream, but he figured they were arguing and would work it out.

The bearded man swooped Kaylen up in his arms, as several other men and women bombarded the house from the front and back.

"Daddy! Daddy! Daddy!" All the girls screamed for their father.

Sue's daughter, Kendall, ran to her father and banged on the door like a wild banshee.

"Daddy's using the bathroom. I'll be out—"

"They takin' us, Daddy! The bad men are in the house and they takin' us!"

Spencer half-wiped his ass, pulled up his pants, and opened the door. He heard the heavy footsteps coming up the stairs. He covered Kendall's mouth and told her, "Be quiet." He ran to Kemoni's bedroom and opened her closet. "Go ahead. Get in and call your mother when you don't hear anyone else in the house."

The small child was shaking and scared. She loved Spencer in the purest form, through a child's eyes. "But daddy, they took Kaylen and—"

"Shhhhh, baby girl. Do like daddy has taught y'all girls a thousand times before. Daddy loves you." Spencer kissed her tear-filled cheek.

"Love you too, daddy." Kendall pulled up the floor space and crawled to the set of steps that led to the attic, where Spencer had a small refrigerator with water and food, and a cell phone with a chip in it, in case someone broke in and he needed to hide anyone or all of his children.

In a matter of minutes the Feds had confiscated his home, money, freedom, and most important, his children.

Spencer born and raised in the streets. No time for love or emotions. His mother and father were both hustlers, and they raised him as such. His father ran numbers and protection for the dope man, while his mother headed a whorehouse, so they taught him every angle of the game. But he knew what his downfall was—pussy, soft curves, big butts, and pretty smiles. And now because of a piece of jealous, conniving, vengeful pussy, he was through. If he could have kept his dick in his pants, he would still have the six-point-seven-million-dollar fortune.

The young correctional tapped on his cell bars. "Spencer Mack, you have a visitor."

CHAPTER 34

Pepper and Emil were already heading to the back of Layla's house to block the back door, as Mo and Koi sat in the rental car and watched Gabby leave out the driveway.

Gabby studied the parked car sitting across the street from her client's house, but Mo turned her face away and she didn't recognize Koi, so she drove on.

Mo hit the steering wheel. "Bitch! I knew it."

"What is it, Moses?" Koi asked sweetly.

Mo jumped out the car. "Listen, stay out of my business. Get into the driver seat and keep the car running. If that lady comes back, or the police or anybody come up to the car asking questions, floor it."

Koi looked at Mo like a confused child on the first day of pre-K. "Floor it? Like get down on the floor?" She smirked.

Mo shook her head. "Like drive the fuck off and don't say shit to nobody!" She answered, already thinking that Koi's dumb ass was going to be a problem. She walked quickly to Layla's door, looking around to make sure no one was out that could identify her.

She hesitated for a second before pressing *end* on her vibrating cell phone, for the hundredth time in the last week. Jovan had not let up yet. She'd told him that she was confused and stressed out, that she just needed a break.

Layla, still wearing a face bandage, moved suitcases and boxes with her feet as she opened the door. She didn't bother to look out the window or peephole. She just assumed it was the blonde-haired, blue-eyed woman again. "What the fuck—"

Mo pushed her inside the house by her sore, freshly-operated-on face.

Layla tripped over a box and hit her forehead on the corner of the sharp-edged coffee table. "Ahhh shit!" she screamed out.

Mo straddled Layla, as Pepper and Emil entered the front door, and squeezed firmly around her neck. "What was that white woman doing here?"

Layla spat in Mo's face.

Mo drew back and swung a closed fist into the bandaged side of her face, splitting some of the stitches. "What was that woman . . . doing here?" she asked as she struggled with Layla.

"That was my aunt—I can't breathe!" Layla tried to free herself from Mo's hold around her neck. If only she could get to the knife on the end of the coffee table, she would end all of the problems.

Pepper and Emil decided to be nosy and search the house, to see why Layla had all the suitcases and moving boxes.

Mo knew she had a fight on her hands, but she was prepared for a battle to the death, if it meant finding out information about getting her and Emil's daughters back. "Layla, this is my last time—"

Layla jerked, almost getting away from Mo.

But Mo grabbed her tighter, choking her until spit began to seep out the sides of her trembling jaws. "Tell me who that woman was . . . before I kill yo' ass!"

Layla stared into Mo's eyes and knew that she was serious about killing her. And why wouldn't she? The blonde lady said that she already had it in the works for Kemoni to be put up for adoption.

Mo reached around her back, ready to end this bitch's life.

Just then Emil came out holding a pink bundle. "Look what I found," she said, cradling the baby in her arms.

The baby began to cry.

That seemed to give Layla the supernatural strength to push Mo off her and onto the floor. She snatched her daughter from Emil and demanded that they get out of her house before she called the police.

All three of them stood looking at Layla like she was a crazy woman. She should have known that they wouldn't leave her presence without knowing why she was holding her child and they couldn't hold theirs.

"I mean it! Get outta my house!"

Mo pulled out the .380 semi-automatic and pointed it at Layla's head. "This is my last time asking you—what was that woman doing here?" She walked up to Layla and placed the gun to the baby's head. The fear on Layla's face looked like she'd seen a monster in a horror film.

Layla screamed as she was backed into the wall, "This bitch is crazy! Y'all make her stop!"

"Look, Mo," Pepper said, trying to find an angle to get between the gun and the baby's head. "It ain't that damn serious."

"It ain't that serious, huh? It ain't that serious?" Mo asked in disbelief that her friend would turn on her. "She got her gotdamn child. Where is mine?" She waved the gun around the room. "Huh, where is mine and Emil's?" Mo wiped the flowing tears from her eyes. She was on the edge, and Layla was just the push she needed to go over.

Emil slowly approached Mo, to not alarm her and have her mistakenly pull the trigger. "We both want our girls back, but we can't get them back in jail."

"So you are who Spencer sent to take me out, dirty bastard!" Layla yelled, making the baby scream even louder. "Y'all deserve each other."

"Spencer? What are you talking about?" Mo looked confused. "Look, I won't hurt you if you just tell me why Gabby was here."

"Gabby? I don't know that white woman's name." Layla gently shook her daughter to calm her down. She just wanted to get to New York and forget about Mo, Spencer, and every other memory of Georgia.

"Look, when you cut my face, Spencer and his flunkies dropped me off at the hospital like damaged goods. That blonde lady came in and asked me a lot of questions. I told her I was out with Spencer and somebody jumped us.

"When she heard Spencer's name, she asked me, was it you who had done this to me. She said she was a counselor for the police department and could help me make you pay without involving Spencer."

"She played your ass," Mo told her. "That lady is the D.A."

"I've been making deals with the D.A. The damn police?"

"You've made deals with the devil."

"How did she help you get your baby back?" Emil asked, not wanting to get lost in a conversation about Mo's worthless, evil mother.

Layla knew she couldn't tell them everything. She began to slowly move closer to the phone. "My mother paid a lawyer for me."

Mo knew it was a lie, but short of shooting her, Layla wasn't going to break. Her text message sounded. She turned to Pepper. "Let's go. The number is almost up."

Before Mo went to Layla's house, she'd set up an alibi by going to the welfare office, grabbing a number, and signing her name. She found a young mother and paid her two hundred dollars to text her when her number got close.

Layla quickly grabbed the phone and dialed 9-1-1.

"Put it down!" Mo demanded.

Layla shook her head no.

Mo lost control and shot the base of the phone, sending pieces flying everywhere.

Emil and Pepper dragged Mo kicking and screaming out the door.

"Let me kill this bitch! She did all this! Hoe, you dead! Dead!"

"Drive, Koi." Pepper shouted. "Pull off!"

"Mo, you better get yo' crazy ass together," Emil told her. "What were you thinking, putting that gun to that baby's head?"

She answered like a small child being reprimanded, "I wasn't."

"Well, you better start."

"I'm sorry that your mother is still doing dirty shit like this to you." Pepper squeezed Mo's hand to let her know that she was there for her.

"Yeah, but she done gone too far this time. I know she had to be the one that helped Layla set Spencer up. But I'll worry about her after we do these hits, get this money and our girls home."

CHAPTER 35

The correctional officer led Spencer to the visiting room. "Yo', son, this bitch is fine as hell, *B*. You better hurry up and get outta here if you wanna keep 'er."

Royal sat at the table with a worried look on her face. Spencer sat down and picked up the phone. He knew this day would come sooner than later. "What's up, ma?"

"Ma." She nervously repeated and laughed. "Boy, would that have sounded good nine years ago."

"I know. I know I fucked up."

She took the picture from her pocket and put it up to the window. "This is what you fucked up."

The snaggle-toothed, brown-skinned, baseball-suit-wearing little boy smiled at Spencer through the picture.

"Damn! He's gotten so big."

"Not big enough that he doesn't need you. I'm tired of pretending that he didn't happen. I'm sick of waiting on you to do the right thing by him. He's asking so many questions." Royal rubbed the perspiration from her forehead. "If all this stuff hadn't happened, I was going to release this pressure off my chest and tell Moses everything."

"She don't have to know anything. It will kill her."

"Kill her? What about King? If a woman can't understand that you had a child before you met her, then you shouldn't want to be with her. I'm not hiding my child no more. I'm bringing him home here with me, once we finish with these hits."

"It's not King that she'll reject, it's his mother. And y'all been tight since y'all were little. Why ruin it now?"

"Being a mother is my first priority. Stop thinking with your dick. Think clearly about this. Mo is going to be pissed at both of us." She hung her head for a moment, thinking about how all this got started. "We were still together while you were seeing her."

Royal had made up her mind. She was definitely going to tell Mo everything. She deserved to know.

"When y'all get this cheese, and I get out, I'm gon' be his daddy full-time, I promise. You just don't know, Royal. I had everything in order. I was going to marry Mo, tell her about King, and live in peace." He shifted in his seat and turned his head so that no one could hear what he was about to say. "I had all seven of my kids a five-hundred-fifty-thousand-dollar trust with a hundred thousand for each of their mothers. Come on, Royal, you know me. Even though I haven't been there like I should have, King never wanted for nothing."

"You, physically." Royal said, pissed at the thought of money taking the place of a father all these years. "You just don't know how my heart broke when I walked in on you and Mo that night. I got my neck sliced because I was more focused on you than saving my own ass." She swallowed the large lump forming in her throat. "You had left me in Newbie thinking that you were coming back for us. And then the one friend that I've always been down for and been down for me, you were making her another baby mama."

Royal shook her head and wiped away years of tears. "That hurt. That hurt a lot. You left me and King out in the cold. I had to leave my baby with Mom's best friend so I could do better for both of us."

"I apologize. I didn't mean to fuck up your life."

"Yeah, well, you live and you learn."

With all of that off her chest, she wiped away the last tear she would shed for her years of hurt and got down to business. "So give me some real info on this Philly connect."

Spencer smiled, thinking that he would love to be there when those two got together. "She real anal, got the heart of a nigga, and she loves a good piece of hot pussy."

"Well, that makes two of us." She smiled at Spencer, teasing his imagination.

"Just play it cool, get in and get out. Y'all should be all right."

"I pray to God that all of these hits pan out. Mo is losing it without Kemoni, and I don't know how much longer she can take it."

"Just be there for her. She trusts you."

Royal bit her lip and sighed. "It's been hard lately. My conscience gets the best of me, and I can't be all fake up in her face."

Spencer understood. He wanted to, and would make it right when he was released. "Okay, okay. Just hold tight for me. I'm gon' take care of all of this when I get out." He got up to leave. "Hey, watch Pig. Watch her close. She a crackhead. She'll turn on y'all. Use her street smarts and let her go. And . . . umm . . . tell 'im I love him."

Royal nodded, and they parted ways. She walked away with a pep in her step. Her son wouldn't be a bastard after all.

CHAPTER 36

Two weeks and three days before Christmas and Mo was determined to get Kemoni home to open her presents. She'd been at the lowest point of depression because the social workers still denied visitation to all the mothers of Spencer's children, deeming them threats to the children's lives.

The lawyer was generous enough to accept the first seven thousand dollars to start the case as a whole because he felt sorry for them all. This was his way of thanking Spencer for paying for a house for him in the Hamptons, a Range Rover, and a nice-size savings. But Mr. Humphries still had to meet with Gabby Cantrell to see why all the girls had court dates except Kemoni and Moses. Their case had been removed from the docket altogether.

As the lawyer did his part, the women prepared to do theirs.

Mo grabbed her duffle bag and looked in Kemoni's room. "This is all for you, baby girl. Mommy loves you."

She closed the pink-and-yellow bedroom door, and her soft heart too.

Emil told Mekia that Pepper had hired her and Koi to be her manager and assistant, and they had to accompany her to an audition out of town. She also convinced her mother to come over and take care of Mekia and the kids for a couple of days.

Ascada sat on her five-thousand-dollar, king-size, one thousand thread count sheet, goose down bed and stared at her worthless expression. She'd pleaded with Hunter to go to counseling, but he refused. He told her that he was preparing to tell his family about Eric and wanted a divorce. She was cut off from everything.

She had no choice but to join The Clique and participate in criminal activity in order to survive.

Pepper was strong, but still miserable without Joc. She didn't know if it was the privileged lifestyle or the man himself. The mafia made it easy for her not to see him. After the fiasco on Thanksgiving, they quickly moved all her stuff into a storage unit and in with Mo. They froze all Joc's accounts, seized all his properties, and moved him to Brazil, alienating him from the world and Pepper. He still sent her whatever he could sneak away. But since his wife disappeared, they were tight on his ass. Pepper heard rumors that he'd killed his wife in the penthouse after torturing her for four days.

Royal rubbed King's back, kissed him on the cheek, and placed his weekly gift on his nightstand. She looked around at his room, at all the sport and art plaques, and paintings he'd done in class that hung on the walls. She'd come in the middle of the night while he slept because, if not, he would give her the third degree of why he couldn't go with her, or why she couldn't stay with him. But after her hit, everything would be all right, and he was coming home with her.

The drive to Columbus, Georgia was short and sweet, but long enough to give the women a chance to discuss last-minute details. Royal and Brooke were on their way to Philly, and Nevada and Pig were already in Miami.

They pulled up to Hilton Gardens, and Emil, Koi, Mo, Pepper, and Ascada walked into the hotel like they were celebrities. All eyes were on them. They had two suites, one for them to sleep and dress, the other to seduce their victims.

"Ascada, you might wanna slow down on the drinks, chick," Pepper told her.

"Do yo' man slow down when he drinks? Ooops." She covered her mouth like she was surprised. "You ain't got a man no more." Ascada laughed aloud.

Mo looked at Pepper with sorrowful eyes. "She's going through it. You remember, right? She really thinks Hunter is coming back to her."

"Yeah, whatever. I'm still going through it too. Where's my sympathy? That bitch better stay out of my way." Pepper dismissed Ascada because she was miserable right now and wanted everyone around her to feel what she was feeling.

Mo snatched the bottle from Ascada. "No more. No drinking on the job." She gulped down the last shot of brandy and sat quietly in the oversized hotel chair, mentally preparing herself for what was supposed to happen over the next month.

Spencer had instructed the ladies to spread out and make the hits at the same time, so the connects wouldn't hear of the others' misfortune and be on the alert. Once Mo was secure that Pepper and Ascada could handle things and weren't vulnerable because of personal feeling, she was flying to Denver. The last hit would involve all of them in New York. After that, they would have enough money to get the girls back, get Spencer out of jail, and retire.

CHAPTER 37

T.I.'s "What You Know about That" pumped throughout the club. The DJ was crunk, and the crowd was hype. Koi, Pepper, and Ascada walked through the door with all the right assets. Koi's bubbly personality, long wavy weave, big ass, and small waist squeezed into a size ten Seven jeans, when she really needed a size fourteen. Pepper's beautiful smile, full lips, and protruding hips demanded attention. And Ascada's smooth skin, petite, tight, S-shaped body, with a nonchalant attitude always made men notice her.

Instantly, two young thugs fitting the description of their intended targets' right-hand men approached them at the bar.

One of the men sported two huge diamonds, his hat to the back, and a drink in his hand. He said to Ascada, "Slim, can a brotha get ta know ya?"

Ascada tossed her hair over her shoulder, making sure he saw her face. "Not a fat chance in hell, slim." She turned back to face the bar and winked at Pepper.

"I don't know, A. They look pretty damn cute to me." Pepper sipped her apple martini.

"That'll be thirty-nine dollars for all three drinks and the one shot," the short, round bartender informed them.

"Let me get that for these beautiful ladies. Matter fact, put it on our tab." The young thug pulled out a fat wad of money.

"Umm, no, I got it." Pepper pulled out her fat wad.

Ascada laughed at the sight of the fake baller wad. It was two hundred-dollar bills, one twenty, five ones, and a bunch of paper.

Pepper eyed the young thug. "How much is your tab?"

Coby wasn't going to be outdone by a chick. He and his crew were the high rollers. Besides, he was really attracted to Slim, who went by the name A.

"Sixty-five dollars right now," the bartender answered.

Pepper slid the hundred-dollar bill to the bartender, and all three of the ladies walked away.

Coby and his partner stared in amazement at the women. They were beautiful, fine and self-assured. He immediately got on his Nextel and chirped the man in charge—their intended target, to let him know they had found fresh, new grade-A meat.

The outside world labeled Columbus, Georgia a small, slow, country town, but inside the city limits were hot, beautiful women, talented athletes, recording stars, and a very profitable drug game. And at the top of the game was CT.

An hour later, as the ladies danced and entertained the local male patrons of the club, CT walked in with an entourage of twelve men and women.

Koi's gold-diggin' ass noticed him first. "I think ya man has arrived. And oooh, girl, he is fine and ballin'!"

It was like a scene straight out of the movies. He walked through the door with "We Fly High" by Jim Jones bumping in the background. It seemed like time stood still. Men and women both rushed this fine man standing in all white and diamonds.

Wise walked thru V.I.P. with no hesitation. He dapped his two homeboys who had approached the three women when they first arrived at the club. Bottles of Dom, Grey Goose, and Patrón started filling the tables in V.I.P.

Pepper took in a deep breath and threw a shot of Hennessy down her throat, to swallow the thick lump that was cutting off her air supply. *I can't believe my eyes. This isn't happening. It's Wise, aka CT. Oh shit! What am I going to do? I got to get outta here.*

"Come on, we gotta go." Pepper grabbed her purse and prepared to pay for their last round of drinks. She scanned the room, and there was no waitress in sight. So she rushed to the bar to settle their tab.

Ascada watched Pepper run around like a chicken with its head cut off, telling them to leave. But she was full of liquor and ready to play. She wasn't going to let Pepper stop her fun, so she called Moses to intercept.

"Yeah, what's up?"

"Pepper is trippin'," Ascada told Mo, as she calmly sipped on her glass.

Mo sat up in the cab that she and Emil shared on their ride to the hotel. "What do you mean, she trippin'?"

"She act like she seen a ghost."

CHAPTER 38

Wise spotted Pepper when he first came in. That's why he paused at the door. His heart weighed his feet down. This was the love of his life. The motivation for his get-money attitude. The force behind the empire he was building. When he saw her jump up and go to the bar with her purse in hand, he knew she was leaving.

Wise instructed his crew, "Aye, hold it down for a few. I got an old debt to settle."

"You need some back-up?" Coby asked.

"Naw, this is long overdue. And I have to be the one to handle it."

His smooth swagger parted the floor as he made his way to the bar. He stared at Pepper for a second before alerting her that he was behind her. She was still as beautiful as ever. He smiled at her shape. He told her that her weight would work out with her full height, and she would be bad. And she was.

He casually leaned his elbows on the bar beside her. "Where you rushin' off to? Your Italian stallion got you on a curfew?"

Pepper wouldn't give him eye contact. She knew it didn't take that long for nobody to get change. All their little front money was almost gone. And now she wouldn't complete her mission because the past had come back to bite her in the ass.

"Come on, Pep, you know I know you. And you damn sho' know me."

When the bartender brought back the change, Wise caught him and laid a thousand-dollar bill in his hand to give back to Pepper. He told him, "Keep her change for your tip and hand her this."

"Just give me my correct change please," Pepper said, tears welling up in her eyes.

Wise laid another thousand dollars into the bartender's hand.

Pepper was drowning with guilt, sorrow, and love. He still held her heart in his hand. *Oh Lord, please save me now. Just lift me up out of here. How could I have been so stupid to choose Joc over Wise. He was the one for me.*

"Please just give me my correct change," Pepper begged the bartender, salty tears now running onto her lips.

This time Wise lay three stacks on top of the two already in the bartender's hand.

"Please stop it," Pepper pleaded. She wiped the tears away from her eyes and face.

Wise had felt her pain. He'd lived it for almost three years now. He had a hole, an empty space in his heart, missing her and longing to feel those juicy, full lips, her thick thighs hugging around his waist, and her whispering, "I love you," with that sweet voice. When he was with Pepper, he was legitimate. And now that he was walking a fine line, he definitely needed and wanted her by his side.

Pepper turned to walk away, but he grabbed her hand. "Don't leave again like this. I'm sorry."

Pepper finally looked at Wise with her big honey-brown

eyes. He almost melted on contact, but had to stay focused because he was in his territory.

Wise laid the five thousand dollars in the bartender's hand the way Joc had laid it in her mother's hand three years ago to have Pepper.

"Get the money, Pep," Wise told her.

"I won't be bought again."

"I'm not trying to buy something that already belongs to me. Get the money, girl."

Pepper grabbed the money out of the bartender's hand, leaving him with an extra four-hundred-dollar tip. "I guess it's both our lucky day."

The bartender smiled at Pepper and nodded his head in agreement.

Ascada saw everything that went down and made a quick call back to Mo and let her know that everything was under control.

"Go get ya girls and meet me at the Hilton. It's right down the street on the left hand side."

"I don't think —"

"I didn't ask you to. Just meet me at the Hilton in thirty minutes." He pinched her chin like he used to when they were dating. That was his special way of saying I love you.

CHAPTER 39

Philadelphia was freezing cold, and there was a light misty rain. But Royal and Brooke still put on their Jackie Onassis, big-eyed shades, pointy-toed stiletto boots, and their short, black minks.

Spencer instructed them to step like "professional Clydesdales" in the latest fashions and hottest attitudes, and the female connect would find them.

Philly ran Philadelphia. That's how she got her name. She was drop-dead gorgeous, a full head of perfect, fluffy, sand-brown hair that was cut to swing right under her chin. Her chinky eyes were like roasted, toasted almonds, while her thin lips housed a perfect porcelain white smile. Her size eight waist could barely keep up with her full hips and bottom. She was the perfect woman, except for the fact that she was hard as the toughest nigga in the dope game.

Philly was a rude, cutthroat female. She'd slice a bitch's face, shoot a nigga in the head, and leave them stanking on their loved one's doorstep. But she had one weakness. Hot fish. When she was occupied with a beautiful, sassy, smart woman who let her take control, she'd lose her business sense.

Royal and Brooke worked the city for two days without a word or signal. But at the end of the third day, while they were at the mall in the Coach store, the salesgirl walked over to them with an offer. "Excuse me, ladies, an admirer has left a twenty-five-hundred-dollar shopping pass for each of you." The petite white lady with a floppy bun on her head smiled at the thought of her commission.

"Bingo!" Royal smiled.

Brooke, knowing that Philly was somewhere watching, leaned over and grabbed Royal's ass, pulling her close, kissing her deep and passionate.

Royal tried to protest, but Brooke held on to her head for dear life.

Philly stood at the top of the escalator watching the women that stirred up conversation all over Philadelphia, her workers blowing up her phone as soon as the girls hit town. But, first, she had to scope them out and make sure they weren't the po-po. "Two for the price of one," she said to herself. She rubbed her pussy through the painted-on Michael Kors jeans.

People passing by gawked at Philly as she openly masturbated.

An older white woman that looked like she'd just jumped out a pot of grease said loudly into Philly's ear, "Go get a room. You should be arrested. How disgustingly sick you are."

"Bitch, you wish someone would touch that funky pussy of yours."

As the woman got on the escalator mean-mugging her, Philly shouted out, "Watch your step," and pushed the lady down the escalator.

To passers-by it looked as if Philly was trying to catch the lady before she fell.

As the white woman screamed out, Brooke and Royal spotted Philly coming down the escalator with a smug look on her face.

"Someone come and help this big bitch get off the floor," Philly yelled, to bring embarrassment to the woman. She spat on the lady as she stepped over her.

Brooke's panties instantly got wet from the power Philly exuded.

Philly snapped her fingers, and two salesgirls came to her. They knew her money well. She dropped at least two thousand every other week. "So, have you ladies picked out some fly shit yet?"

"Yes, Miss *P*," one of the younger salesgirls responded.

"Wine and cinnamon biscottis for these fine ladies."

The other young saleswoman removed Philly's boots and began to massage her feet before retrieving the latest stock for her to try on.

Brooke was very attracted to Philly, and the feeling was mutual. But Philly was smitten with Royal. Her smooth, dark skin and glass-gray eyes made Philly's pussy thump. She wanted to eat that fat ass right there on the spot.

Brooke took advantage of the moment and slid her hand between Royal's legs because she knew at this critical point, in front of Philly, she wouldn't and couldn't reject her.

Royal wanted to slap the shit out of Brooke, but something inside of her awoke at the sight of Philly and her rough, harsh attitude. She knew she wasn't gay, because she still couldn't eat coochie, but her freaky side was definitely awakened by this sexy woman.

After going on a mini shopping spree, spending eight thousand dollars of Philly's money, Philly took them to dinner at Mocha's, a five-star restaurant that served priceless entrées.

"So what brought you guys to Philly?" She was talking about herself more than the city.

They both started and stopped at the same time. "We—"

"Business venture," Royal told her.

"What kind?" Philly inquired, trying to see what kind of help she could give Royal, to let her know she had her back in more ways than one.

"A boutique or two. Maybe a strip club."

As Philly finished her favorite meal, spaghetti and meatballs, she raised her eyebrow. "Strip club? My kinda business. Can you dance?" She pointed her fork at Royal, making sure Brooke didn't speak.

"Definitely."

"I would love to see how that big juicy ass move." She flicked her tongue at Royal.

Royal smiled and flirted at the idea, while Brooke twisted uncomfortably in her chair, clearing her throat to let them both know that they were going too far.

"Have you gotten any investors yet?" Philly asked, reeling her big fish in.

"No." Royal shook her head, faking disappointment, as she played in her salad.

"Well, I like it like that anyway. Only one to share with." She looked Brooke dead in the eyes. "How much do you want?"

"We need—"

"Want."

Philly's pretty smile made Royal blush, but made Brooke cringe with fear of losing Royal. "Excuse me?" Royal asked, confused.

"If you with me all your needs are met every day of your life. All I need to know is your wants."

Royal scooted her chair close as Brooke's arm hung on to it. "And what do I have to do to get all of this?"

Philly wiped her mouth with her napkin and spoke soft

and sensual. "Let me eat that thang at will and guide you into the life of luxury and lust."

Royal snatched her chair from Brooke and moved it right up to Philly's chair. She leaned in, sliding her hand between Philly's thighs. "You can slide that pretty tongue of yours across my wet clit anytime your heart desires."

Brooke jumped up from the table and slammed down her drink. "I'm not going along with this shit anymore. I'll be waiting at the hotel to leave."

At this point, Royal wanted Philly to herself. Having a beautiful, soft, powerful woman suck on her clit was an added bonus to the money.

CHAPTER 40

The cold, beautiful snow slowly trickled down onto Mo and Emil's face. They'd never seen so much snow before in their life, living in the Dirty South. They played around like kids, throwing snowballs at each other, laying down in the deep snow and making snow angels.

For a few hours they were free of the heavy burdens of the girls, Spencer, Gabby, bills, and Denver, the rich, white boy they were there to rob.

Denver was an rich, arrogant white boy. Raised in Africa, he came from old, long money, but had short patience and compulsive habits that exposed him as an easy target.

He owned ski resorts and restaurants to wash up his dope money. Dutch Ice was his number one resort, as well as his home. He built his eleven-thousand-square-foot home on top of his biggest moneymaker.

It'd been four days since Mo and Emil left the girls in Columbus, Georgia, and they were already in. They pulled him in on the first day they were playing in the snow. He was attracted to any woman that wasn't Caucasian. But he loved the browner sugar.

Denver greeted Emil as she exited the elevator to his home. "Emil, you look like something out of my dreams."

Emil was speechless at the sight of his grand home. The floors were glass with stripes of what looked like snow. And at the push of a button, for complete privacy, he could frost the entire floor. She took her seat at his round dinner table. "You look nice also."

Emil wanted to hurry up and get it over with. Sleeping with someone you know and like is one thang, but sleeping with a man that you're not attracted to is a mutha. Denver's teeth looked like he hadn't brushed them since he got them. His skin was oily, his hair was greasy, and the dingy, tattered clothes he wore reeked of musk and animal scent.

She smiled and played her part. Giggling and playing an airhead, she got him to open up and tell all his secrets about his money and jewels. He was so gone on Emil's charm that he even told her where he hid the money and jewels in his home.

After a long, six-course meal, Emil was now the dessert. He led her to a red, exotic room filled with leopard and zebra print rugs, curtains, and bedspread. Expensive vases and African artifacts lined the dressers and walls. Denver left her alone and went to the bathroom.

Emil ran her fingertips along the edge of the large elephant tusk. She touched the fur of the African drum.

"Rahhhhhh!" Denver jumped out of a secret passage in the wall, holding something balled up in his hand. "Uh uh uh." He cupped her hand into his with a little pressure. "These things are too expensive for touching."

Oh Lord, he gon' kill me. He gon' cut my ass up and put me on the wall next to the buffalo butt. Is that sweat on his forehead? Is he deranged? Mo better get her ass up here and save me from this paranoid schizophrenic.

"Is your dope in the safe too?"

He lifted his wet face and looked at her spacy for a second.

Oh shit! Has this crazy fool overrode the power of the film?

"Down there." He pointed to the floor.

Emil looked all around the floor but saw only glass. "Down where, baby?" she asked, confused.

"Jus' let me eat this sweet pie."

She caught his face in her hand. "Tell mama where and I'll turn around and let you have some chocolate cake."

Denver pointed to the snow-looking stripe in the glass floor.

Emil stared at the floor, putting her hand under chin. Then her eyes lit up. *You smart sucka you. Genius!* "How do I open them?"

"Just stick your finger down the crest and lift up." He whined like a child, "now give me my chocolate cake."

Emil looked at the million-dollar floor, tears in her eyes. "My baby coming home."

"Yeah, baby, I'ma make you cum." He bent her over, slid the thong out of her ass, and dug his face in her chocolate cake.

This time she closed her eyes and enjoyed the ecstasy she was receiving from the tongue, and all the money.

Mo opened the door and watched in shock as Emil held her eyes closed, shook her ass, and came on Denver's face. She placed her empty duffle bag on the floor, looked at her watch. It was going on two hours since Emil had been with Denver, and he still wasn't knocked out. She snuck up behind him and shot a needle full of sleeping medicine in his neck, and he hit the floor with a hard thud.

They quickly pulled him into the bed just as his bodyguards opened the door.

"Is everything all right, *D*?" Mo was sitting on his chest facing toward the front pretending she was giving him

But when she thought about all the money she was about to get and being able to see her daughter, Denver began to look like Robin Thicke, the white R&B singer.

"Put this on." Denver held out a cheetah print, crotchless, one-piece thong with the nipples cut out.

This muthafucka is a true redneck, white boy with chocolate dreams. Just think about Kaylen, Emil. Think Kaylen. "Umm, baby, can we have some wine?" She kissed him passionately on his thin, pale lips so that he would get the drink ASAP.

He stood motionless, kissing the air well after she'd stepped away. "You are so damn sweet." He pushed a button on the huge, square remote control, and one of the walls spun around to reveal a large round stage complete with pole, mirrors, disco ball, and a long mink coat.

What the fuck is all this? This crazy fool is gon' turn me into a monkey for real. I told Mo he looked like one of those deranged suckas you see on America's Most Wanted *that liked to fuck animals and shit.*

He popped her on the ass. "Get on up there and show me what you working wit'."

Emil thought she was going to be sick. His yellow stained teeth seemed to be glowing as the disco ball spun around. "That big drink please."

"Nurse mine until I come back."

This was going to be easier than she thought. Her overnight bag was already in the room, sitting in a chair next to the outfit he'd bought her. She rushed over to it and then stopped in her tracks. Her heart was beating fast. *What if he got surveillance?* She turned her head like the exorcist, looking in every direction, and every corner of the room. *Okay, Emil, take long, steady, slow, deep breaths. Not now, don't start now.* She closed her eyes, put her hand on her chest, and thought about Kaylen.

Emil had been dealing with anxiety attacks since Walsh,

but she pretty much had them under control, until she found herself in tight situations. She slowly reached in her bag and grabbed the small film. She then took a sip of his drink and, at the same time, slid the almost invisible film into the drink.

Royal was the mastermind behind the small, clear films. She'd learned about them in pre-med chemistry lab. They were a mixture of truth serum, ecstasy, date rape drug, and memory eraser. She also put it into liquid form, to be given as a shot.

The truth serum and ecstasy lasted an hour and then the HB kicked in for at least six. And the memory eraser was uncertain. It could erase from two days before, the actual day of the event, or nothing at all. She was pulling up her last strap when Denver returned with a glassy, dazed stare on his face.

He was beating on his chest and yelling, "Ahhhhhhh. Me Tarzan, you Jane." He handed Emil the orange juice and vodka, took his drink back, and gulped it down.

She sat her drink down, not wanting to drink anything she couldn't see him pour, and nervously walked to the stage and began to move around. As she dipped down to the ground and gyrated her hips, he pulled out his extra, extra long and wide speckled dick and began to stroke it.

This shit is not happening. This asshole better fall out quick 'cause that freckled pecker ain't sliding up in me.

As Emil bent over to show him the hole in her crotch, he said, "Open that fat black ass up and let me see that pink bunny rabbit."

She did as he asked. "How much would you pay for this pussy, baby?"

"All the money in that safe." He pointed to the adjacent wall with all the African artifacts on it.

Yep, he's gone. Time to go to work.

As he masturbated like she wasn't in the room, she re-trieved her cell phone and text messaged Mo to co the room. Denver had slipped when he allowed Mo to in one of his guestrooms.

Emil sat on his lap, spat into the palm of her hand, began to rapidly stroke his enormous penis.

"Ooooh yeah, that's why I love you black bitches. know how to please a man."

"You white pecker wood. What's the combination that safe?"

"Talk dirty to me, bitch. I love it like that." He began t slobber.

"Combination, prick."

Unaware of what was going down, he was in hog heaven. "Thirty-eight, twenty-eight, forty-two, the mea-surements of what I like sitting on my dick."

"How much is in it?"

"Get on yo' knees and suck my dick till you bleed it dry, ho." He was coming up out of his seat with excitement.

"Hold on, daddy. Let this pussy marinate first." *Come on, Mo. Damn! This horny fool gon' try to bust me wide open if you don't come on.*

He unexpectedly and quickly flipped Emil into the chair, got on his knees, pushed her ass to the top of the chair, and spread her legs. Before she could protest, his thick tongue was lapping her middle.

Damn! What they say about white boys is definitely true. Even though I'm gon' have to pop a Diflucan when I get home because of that caked-up bacteria on his filthy yellow teeth. Mama is going t enjoy this.

He ate Emil's pussy like it was the last of his favorit dish. Letting the feeling take over, and forgetting who wa between her legs, she grabbed his greasy, moussed ha and pushed his face deeper. "Mmmm, hell yeah! Swall them juices." She held herself steady as Denver we crazy, almost pushing her over the chair.

head, as Emil sat on his face. Mo pushed his hand up in the air to signal everything was straight.

"Lucky bastard," one of the guards said to the other.

Mo ran and locked the door. "So where is the dope?"

"In the floor."

"In the floor?" Mo asked, her top lip turned up.

Emil bent down on her knees and pulled open one of the frosted stripes. The twelve-foot-long, six-inch-deep stripes were full to the brim with cocaine.

"Get a cup out of the bathroom and start putting it in the bags while I raid the safe," Mo said to Emil.

They swept Denver out in less than twenty minutes. They set their timers and slept for four hours, for rest, and so that it wouldn't look suspicious to the guards. They would be able to leave when the guards did a shift change. Mo shot Denver with one more dose of sleep medicine then dreamed about her reunion with her daughter.

CHAPTER 41

Something was definitely wrong on Thursday morning, before Christmas Day, as Mo, Emil, and Nevada sat at the Humphries law firm. They had been finished with their hits a week and a half ago. Royal and Brooke checked in and said they were wrapping up a hit, which should have already been finished. But neither Pepper nor Ascada was answering their cell phones, and when Mo called the hotel, they had already checked out. And, on top of all that, their lawyer was acting shady.

The black-haired, clean-cut, thousand-dollar-suit, platinum-cufflink-wearing lawyer opened the thick folder. "Ladies, we have a problem."

"For eighty-four thousand dollars there shouldn't be any missing commas or periods."

The lawyer sighed and reclined in his heated turbo massage chair. He'd dealt with all kind of cases before and never felt an ounce of remorse for charging his clients so much money. If they'd just paid attention to detail, read a book every once in a while, the majority of them wouldn't need a lawyer to handle these simple cases.

But this time, Judge Cantrell and D.A. Gabby White-Cantrell were breaking his balls on this case. It was like they had a personal vendetta against these girls, Mo especially.

"I thought we would have the girls home by now, but DFACS has messed up the processing files and sent Nevada's to New York. And Mo's has to be re-issued to the courts."

"That sounds like a bunch of bullshit!" Mo said through clenched teeth.

"Ms. Whyte, I assure you—"

"Your expensive ass assured me when I laid that first ten thousand in your hand and you told me a definite yes when I gave you the other money." Mo scooted to the edge of her seat. "Because Spencer is locked up doesn't mean his presence can't be felt on the street. I'm sure you know all too well how this works."

Emil looked at the unfamiliar woman sitting next to her that she called her best friend. Mo was fading fast and this beast was left to be by their side. She was rude, cocky, and had no restraint when it came to her anger.

"Let me assure you—"

"No, Mr. Humphries, let me assure you. You're dealing with an angry clique of women this time around, overemotional, tired, stressed-out, detached mothers."

All three of them raised up at the same time.

"We suggest you take care of this so-called problem and get our babies home, or your babies"—Mo pointed to the picture of three little boys on his desk—"won't have a daddy to come home to."

Standing outside the lawyer's office, the beast came out in raw form. Pacing back and forth like a wet hen Mo said, "That bitch better get my gotdamn child by Monday or I'm shooting up his fucking office and his house."

Nevada pleaded with her, "Moses, please calm down. Let's think rationally right now."

Mo's eyes got big, her heart began to race, and her mouth became dry. She rushed Nevada, pushing her head into the red brick building. "Bitch, how dare you try and tell me how to feel about my only child." Mo pushed her elbow deep into Nevada's neck. "I owe you an ass-whuppin' anyway!"

"Quit it! Just stop it!" Emil yelled. She snatched Mo by the same arm that she had Nevada pinned to the wall with. "We don't need this shit right now! All of us are going thru the same thing. I wish you would stop acting like Kaylen is the only child DFACS took." Emil let go of Mo and stuck her freezing hands back into her wool coat. "We need to find out where the hell Pepper, Ascada, and Koi are. Mekia is becoming suspicious. He keep askin' me where his cousin is."

Without acknowledging any of what Emil said about her attitude, Mo continued with her rampage. "I knew we shouldn't have left Pepper in charge, by herself. Not right now, after Joc." Mo headed to her Hummer, Emil and Nevada close on her heels.

Emil wanted this to all hurry up and be over with so she could have her friend back.

Ring, ring!

Mo snatched the phone from the dashboard and answered it without looking at the caller ID. "Y'all better be on the way home."

"Everything good up here. We should be wrapping it up in another week or so."

"Week or so?" Mo said with an attitude. She wanted all money accounted for, in case she had to shell out more to the lawyer to get her baby back.

"That's what I said. This bitch ain't playing. She ain't gon' just let nobody up in her space that quick. I'm working her. I know how to handle mine," Royal said, sensing the aggression in Mo's voice. "I'll holla at you in a couple of days." And she was gone.

"Have you guys talked to Pig?" Nevada asked nervously, wanting to break the tension.

"Hell no." Mo looked at Nevada through the rearview mirror. "I'm glad that's over and done with with her." She watched Nevada nervously twist her hair. She knew something wasn't right. "Why you ask?"

Nevada didn't want to be the bearer of bad news and tell them that Pig was completely strung out and had already spent all her money. "I thought she would be around asking for more money by now."

Mo knew something else was up with her asking about Pig.

When Mo and Emil went to collect money from one of Spencer's trap houses, a runner had already informed them about Pig's activities. "Aye, yo', y'all be careful out here." The young hustler continuously looked over his shoulder. "Word on the street is a clique of honeys is straight gankin' niggas, anybody in the game."

"Oh yeah?" Emil wanted to know how much info was on the street. "Any idea who the girls are?"

"Naw, but they gon' get this"—he patted the gun strapped to his hip—"up in they pussyhole if they come 'round here wit' dat shit." He spat on the ground to show his disgust for what the clique of women was doing.

"Where you hear that from?" Emil asked, wanting to keep a tab on the information source.

"What's that ho name that be wearin' all those crazy-ass hair colors?" He snapped his fingers, trying to remember her name. "Um . . . um . . . um . . . Piggy. Yeah, Piggy."

"Pig." Mo tightly gripped the steering wheel and rose up in her seat.

"Yeah, yeah, Pig, that's it. She was 'round the way the

other day, trying to score some free dope. And when my boys shunned her away, she started yelling 'bout she was part of 'em and they was taking over the game and shit."

"You know that hoe dizzy, neighborhood crack ass," Emil said, insuring damage control.

"Man, she was high as hell. That bitch had her bra on the outside of her shirt and was slobbering out the mouth. If she wasn't Spencer baby mama, we would have did her ass in broad daylight."

"Next time, you got my permission to take that bitch out."

They laughed it off, but Mo and Emil knew that they had to put a stop to Pig or she would ruin everything. She fucked with a lot of young, up-and-coming dope boys, and it was only a matter of time before she let the cat out of the bag.

CHAPTER 42

"Get ch'all damn ass somewhere and sit down!"
"We thirsty. We hungry," the children chanted.

"Drank yo' spit and chew on ya gotdamn tongues!" Pig yelled over a Jay-Z mixed CD she was blasting. "Now get the hell outta here!" She flung a half full bag of Cool Ranch Doritos chips onto the floor. Then she slumped her high, unwashed, pregnant body onto an infested leather sectional that housed, filth, crushed M&Ms, macaroni shells, and bread crumbs. "Y'all bastards stay in that room until I tell you to come out."

She slid a brown suitcase from underneath the dirty, worn-out cream sectional and lay it on the wobbly coffee table. She spread a wide line of cocaine on the cracked table, but in her haste, a huge portion of it fell to the floor. She dived like a champion swimmer to the nasty carpet, took one long sniff, pinched her nose, and blew.

Pig, looking like the "Pillsbury Doughgirl," fell back against the sofa, her eyes rolling back in her head. Her mind began to spin out of control, thinking about how she ended up strung out on drugs, four children with a different daddy for each of them, on welfare, selling her body, and no self-worth.

Pig's mother was a hot girl on a roll, and the small town she grew up in knew it. Pastors, husbands, even cousins, could get a piece of Sweet Pea's pie. But when she got pregnant and had Pig, from God knows who, she blamed Pig for everything.

Sweet Pea turned to drugs, robbing and prostituting. Anytime Pig would cry, she would fill her bottle formula with powdered milk and cocaine, heroin, alcohol, or whatever was on the floor next to the bed to make her shut up.

Pig learned how to suck dick at the age of two and received her first wienie at four. After a couple of months of trying every drug on the street, Sweet Pea was strung out. Before Pig, the drugs, and the men, she was a scholar, so she home-schooled Pig, to make money off her at the same time.

There was no escape for Pig, no grandmother, auntie, or social worker. She survived the best way her mother showed her—dope men. They provided the dividends, the dope, and the dick.

Pig was definitely nasty, ghetto, and strung out, but she had a good shot between her thighs and all the dope boys on the grind hit it relentless.

Ding-dong! Ding-dong!

Pig stumbled to the door, knocking her thigh into the sharp, jagged edge of the raggedy sofa, cutting a deep gash that she was numb to. She opened the door and walked back to the sofa without looking to see who it was.

"Why you got that damn music up so loud?" Kay, her second child's father, yelled over the music.

She ignored him, bobbing her head to the mixed CD, her eyes closed.

Kay walked over to the sofa, parted her legs with his feet, and unbuckled his pants, letting them drop to his ankles. He stroked his dick rapidly to get himself erect. Then he reached over and aggressively snatched Pig's head to him and beat his heavy, AIDS-infected dick on her lips, for her to "open sesame."

Pig opened her hot, unbrushed mouth, and took him down her throat.

The entire time he roughly fucked her mouth, Pig kept her eyes closed, but her eight-year-old daughter, Kaja, kept her eyes wide open, watching as Kay pulled out and skeeted all over her mother's face.

Kay coaxed Pig into telling him everything about the robberies, money, and dope. He grabbed half of her last stack of cash and a Ziploc bag full of coke and went out the front door without saying hello or goodbye to his son.

Kaja ran and jumped face down onto the pissy twin-size mattress that she shared with her brother and cried her little sorrow-filled heart out. She wanted her daddy and her nanna. She wish she was over at her daddy's house the day her sisters were taken. She would have run and jumped in the DFACS people's arms.

Why did her mommy's eyes always look dead, and her hair the color of crayons? And why were so many different men in and out of the smelly, dingy apartment they called home? And why did she have to share a mattress with her little pissy brother and the roaches that seemed to love to crawl into her thick, bushy hair and then fall out as she sat in class reading from her honors book?

She wanted to go and stay with Moses or Emil and be their daughter, wear pretty, pink dresses, ribbons in her hair, and clean, white, ruffle socks with shiny patent leather shoes that click-clacked like a tap dancer's when she walked.

Sometimes when Pig was "riding the high horse," she would send them to school three and four days with the same clothes, no baths, and wild hair. *The next time Moses or Emil comes over here, I'm gon' hide in their car and run away with them. I want to do my homework without a candle or loud, cussin' music in my ear.*

CHAPTER 43

Gerald Levert played softly as Pepper lay on Wise's chest. She flexed her toes back and forth on top of his. He squeezed her close to his chest, her tiny, delicate hand in his big protective one.

He'd missed the hell out of her for close to three years, and he wasn't letting her go again. "When your girls goin' home and leavin' you here with me?" He pulled her on top of him. That beautiful smile, those intoxicating eyes, and that sultry voice was all he needed to get through life.

"What do you mean, when they goin' home? I'm goin' too."

"Nooo, nooo way, beautiful. I'm keeping you here. I got you, and you don't have to worry about money, a job, car, clothes, nothing."

Chills ran down Pepper's spine. She quickly sat up and looked for a way to disappear into thin air. She'd thrown her and Ascada's cell phone down the toilet a week ago and found Ascada and Koi worthy companions until she was ready to make the hit.

Wise realized the anxiety in Pepper's mood. "Sweetness, what's the problem?"

She had tears in her eyes. She wanted to stay, be in true love, and have his babies. Was this world playing a cruel game on her? Why did she have to be the one always losing out? In order to pull this thang off, she would have to go along with what he wanted.

Just a few more days and then we can take him out. But I love this man. I need him, want him. Damn it, Mo and Emil, didn't y'all get enough money on y'all own?

Wise scooted up behind Pepper and wrapped his legs around her. He kissed her back, up to her neck, then pulled her into his chest. "Sweetness, please stay and let me take care of you, be your man."

Pepper knew she had no choice, if she wanted to pull everything off. "Okay, baby, I'll stay."

"Yes!" He kissed her all over, making true promises to always be there and take care of her.

Another week had passed and Pepper had convinced Ascada and Koi not to tell Mo that she knew where the money and drugs were. If only what she'd told them was the truth. They could be ghost with the money and drugs and she could pretend that Ascada and Koi turned on her. She could then stay with Wise and live happily ever after.

But the truth was, Wise had his shit sewed up tight. It was almost like he wasn't selling drugs. The money seemed to just fall from the sky. The only lead she truly had was a storage unit on Buena Vista Road that he stopped by before he took her to the Mercedes dealership.

He'd moved Pepper and the girls from the hotel into his seven-thousand-square-foot, custom-built house, bought her a Mercedes ML500, a new cell phone, and put thousands on a Visa card for her and her girls to eat and shop.

Wise brought Pepper deeper into his life, telling her that

he had a daughter a year earlier, and that she was very sick with sickle cell, and since neither he nor the mother had insurance, he had to foot the entire hospital bill every time she went in.

All of this left Pepper feeling confused. She wanted to stay, but could she really trust that he wouldn't play get-back games with her, because she left him to be with Joc. And then there was Joc. Did she still love him? Would she leave Wise again if Joc came calling?

Ascada walked into the kitchen clutching a silver goblet that she'd made her sixth finger, as Pepper sat at the breakfast bar writing Wise a farewell letter.

"I'm out of Patrón. Can you ask Wise to send for some more?"

Pepper looked at Ascada in disgust. She'd become a drunken slut in less than a month. For every bottle she consumed for dinner, a dick was sure to follow for dessert. "He already sent twice this week for some more."

They locked eyes, exchanging nasty words that didn't need to leave their lips to know what each was saying.

"I'm a grown-ass woman, and I damn sho' don't need your permission—"

"Kill that noise, Ascada." Pepper dropped her pen, mad and frustrated about everything she was facing. "And since you've gotten here, all you've done is drown yourself in a bottle, thinking that's going to make your problems go away."

"Bitch, you don't know nothing about me." Ascada waved the half-empty mug in Pepper's face. "You 'round here actin' like yo' shit don't stank, frontin' in front of that nigga."

Just then, they heard the alarm beep. They looked up at the monitor and saw Wise coming in.

"Maybe, I'll just let him in on your little secret and see if you still be ridin' on that high horse."

Ascada turned to walk and meet Wise, but Pepper caught her by the back of the hair and snatched her slim body down hard onto the marble floor.

"Let me go, you dumb bitch!" Ascada twisted and turned her body, trying to free herself.

Pepper reeled back and slammed her fist into Ascada's face. "Stupid ho, who you think you fuckin' with?"

Ascada slung the red mug wildly into the air, slamming it into Pepper's mouth.

Pepper let go of Ascada and grabbed her mouth as blood shot out.

As the teakettle on the stove whistled, Ascada dragged herself to the stove.

Wise walked through the door. "What the hell is going on in here?" He walked up to Pepper and touched her bloody split lip.

"That drunk, dizzy broad done got beside herself." Pepper pushed Wise's hand away from her mouth. "It probably looks worse than it is." She turned to walk out the kitchen. She was done with everything and everyone. She wanted to break all ties with The Clique and Wise.

"Bitch, since you think you so hot," — Ascada threw the boiling water on Pepper's back — "marinate, hoe."

Pepper let out a loud shrilling scream and dropped to the floor.

Koi, wrapped in a small towel and fresh dick on her breath, ran into the kitchen. She looked at Pepper's wet, steaming back, then at Ascada holding the stainless steel teakettle and knew she had to make that phone call to Mo. "Oh my God, what have you done?"

CHAPTER 44

Everything seemed to be spiraling out of control for the clique and anyone close to them.

That was holding true for Gabby Cantrell as well.

As Robert Cantrell sat hooked up to his dialysis machine, in his mahogany Paul Bunyan bed, he could hardly breathe. He couldn't believe his eyes. How could someone be so cold? The pictures and documents that lay before him had to be a lie. His new wife couldn't have borne a black child. The same black child that was responsible for his broken hip, collapsed lung, and acute renal failure.

She had set the whole thing up. She had him so hoodwinked that while she was pretending to help him get justice for what the clique had done to him, she was stealing his money and property, using his authority to punish her own child, and setting him up to take the blame for all the illegal activities they had done, at the same time, getting him disbarred from the bench and taking over herself.

Cantrell coughed roughly into the phone. "Hey, I need you."

"You got it, Judge," the slow, gruff voice responded. "Who is it this time? Another black chick?"

"I told you, never speak of that," Cantrell said forcefully. "Now listen here." Cantrell explained detail by detail the gruesome acts he wanted carried out. "And I want it delivered to Moses Whyte."

"Robert."

"Damn, boss, she musta really did something to piss you off."

"Just get it to Moses Whyte. Your money will be in the safe deposit box like always."

"Robert, Robert," the angelic voice sang.

He quickly scattered the documents around and pushed the photos into his leather briefcase.

Gabby opened the door, smiling, playing the role of the good wife. "Robert, you didn't hear me calling you?"

"Don't you see I got this damn oxygen mask on my face?"

"Well, honey, everything has been taken care of. Spencer will be caught up in the system for at least three years." She walked to the side of the bed where all the machines were running. She squeezed through a tiny opening and slid next to Cantrell. "And Kemoni will be adopted by the new year. All those black hussies will be broke and jobless for the rest of their lives. We did it, baby!"

Gabby pulled Cantrell to her chest and stroked his balding head.

He wanted to spit in her face, scratch her eyes out, beat her to a pulp so that she had to depend on oxygen for the rest of her life.

"I know what will make you feel a lot better." Gabby took her top off, took his mask off, and replaced it with the nose tube. "Here, baby." She stuck her fake double D breast into his mouth.

He sucked on it like a hungry baby, running his fat, stubby fingers up her skirt and into her pussy.

Nasty, pale, baldheaded, impotent, fat fuck! The things I've put up with since I've married you. How in the hell did you think a young, beautiful, and intelligent woman such as myself would want to be with you without a price tag attached? So I guess I should add dumb and delirious to the list. Gabby pinched the oxygen tube with the heel of her shoe, cutting off Cantrell's air supply.

He let go of her breast and began to gasp for air.

"Here, darling." Gabby put the mask back on and filled the medicine cup with a deadly poison. "Breathe slow and easy, Robert. Take it all in." She snatched his leather briefcase and pulled out the pictures of her and Mo, and Mo's birth certificate. "You didn't think I would know that you had a detective investigating, following me?"

Cantrell punched the air with lazy arms. His heartbeat was faint, and his breathing became shallow.

"I knew you would be too smart for your own good." She snatched the mask off his face.

"Ahhhh . . ." Cantrell felt his heart giving out. He knew he was dead for sure.

"Die already, you fat bastard!" She slapped his beet-red face hard and laughed like a mad woman. "I have everything I've ever wanted, thanks to you—a daughter, all your money, properties, and your seat on the bench. When I take all this evidence to the Supreme Court and show them that you set these poor girls up, I will be deemed a hero and a grieving widow. I will raise Kemoni to be the daughter that Mo could never be."

After Gabby had Mo her life went through the ringer. Her parents cut her out of the will, and no man with any status or money wanted to date her with a black child on her hip.

Gabby heard footsteps coming up the winding staircase. "Help me! Help me!" she screamed, pretending to give Cantrell CPR.

The daily nurse rushed in and assisted her, but it was too late.

CHAPTER 45

It'd been a week since Pepper had entered the hospital, and she was healing beautifully, or so Wise thought. After seeing about her for the entire week, missing money, and not seeing his daughter, he knew this was what he wanted. He wanted to be with Pepper, get custody of his daughter, and leave the streets alone.

He kissed her on the forehead and told her he had to tie up a couple of things and would be back to pick her up and take her home with him.

Pepper cried like a baby. She knew this would be her last time looking him in the face.

"What's wrong, baby girl? You in pain?"

"No. Just happy to be here with you." She hugged his neck.

"You act like you not gon' see me no more or some-thing." He kissed her forehead again, then her chin, and walked out the door.

Pepper wanted something physical from him to keep with her always. "Wait." She slid out of the bed, dragging her IV. "I love you."

"I love you too." He felt something wasn't right, but he couldn't pinpoint it.

"Can I have one of those to wear while you're gone, you know, to feel you still here with me?"

"Sure, baby." He took out his right three-carat diamond earring and put it in her ear, kissed it, and left her for what he thought would be an hour, but would end up being an eternity.

Pepper balled up in the bed and cried like a baby. It was over, and she had to leave him now, after what she'd done.

CHAPTER 46

"Tonight is the night. It's time to go," Brooke said with an attitude. She kicked a pair of thousand-dollar boots into the wall.

"Yeah, yeah, tonight." Royal modeled one of the twenty outfits Philly had bought her the day before.

Brooke sat sulking on the bed, lusting for the body of the woman that she thought was the baddest bitch in the world. "Why do you like her so much?"

Picking up a wide, cream Chanel belt, Royal pictured Philly in her mind. "I like who she is. Her strength."

"Oh, and you don't like who I am?" Brooke asked, tears in her eyes.

Royal sucked her teeth and rolled her eyes. "Look, you knew coming into this what it was." Becoming annoyed with Brooke's insecurities and whining, Royal snatched off her Michael Kors outfit and headed to the bathroom.

"Are you still going to try and see her after all this is said and done?"

Royal didn't answer. She jumped in the shower and mentally prepared for the night. She had no clue where any money or dope was. She was going to have to rely strictly on the truth serum, and pray that it wasn't far from Philly's house.

Philly had her bedroom decked out in yellow and silver, Royal's favorite colors. She wanted everything to feel like home, so that Royal would stay, and send Brooke's cock-blocking ass packing. She knew she could give Royal the world.

Philly grew up with an African father and twelve mothers. Her father brought his beliefs and his eleven wives to America, met her Haitian mother, fell in love, and made her wife number twelve.

When she was only fifteen, she ran away from home because he still ruled with African beliefs. He had cut her clit and sewed up her vagina a year before, when he'd found her in bed with the neighbor's daughter eating her pussy.

Philly felt she was born gay, not turned gay by society or another person, like the world often thought of gay youth. She'd felt feelings for women ever since she could remember feeling anything at all. And she was really feeling Royal, in love with that exotic Amazon. And tonight she was going to pull out all the stops to keep her there.

"How's the crab, Brooke? Snapping?"

Brooke cut her eyes at Philly, knowing she was trying to get on her bad side, make her upset so she would leave and she could have Royal to herself. But not tonight. The only way she was getting her outta there is if she hit her over the head and dragged her out.

Ring, ring, ring!

Philly's ringing phone had been ignored all night until now. "Been waiting patiently. A hundred thousand at midnight."

Royal's eyes got big. She looked at Brooke, Brooke looked at her; they knew Philly was making a deal.

"In one week four million. That's a bet. Yeah, of course. Later." Philly hung the phone up, a smile on her face. "Excuse me, lady and Brooke, where were we?"

Philly continuously caressed Royal's back, thighs, and breasts as they ate, and Royal had no objections. "I got a surprise for you, beautiful." Philly kissed her before leaving the table.

Brooke grunted, feeling nauseous. "Hurry up and stick this bitch so we can go home."

"If she was riding your ass, would you want to go home? Nope. Your gold-diggin' ass would be in heaven."

"Hell yes, I would want to go home. I wouldn't disrespect my woman for a little money and attention."

"You said the magic words, baby, *my woman*, something I don't have."

Philly walked in holding a two-week-old blue pit with a big bowtie around its neck. "A baby for my baby."

"Thank you." Royal freely kissed Philly first.

As the puppy wiggled around, a jangling noise came from its neck.

"What's this?" Royal pulled the bow off, and a ring and key slid off the yellow bow.

"Oh hell naw. Look, we—"

"Accept. What is the key for?" Royal asked.

"For my heart, house, and my honey." Philly stood up and walked to another room and retrieved a pink suitcase and a brown pouch. "What are you going to name the puppy?" She sat the suitcase on the floor.

"King." Royal playfully kissed the puppy.

"Perfect. Let's go to the bedroom."

Royal eyed the suitcase and jumped up with spunk. "Hold on." She went to her purse and took two objects out.

Brooke was happy they didn't have to sleep with Philly. She just knew Royal was going to stick her in the back of the neck right now.

"By all means, Brooke, excuse yourself if you like."

Brooke thought, *Fuck you.*

Royal stuck a piece of gum in her mouth and offered Brooke a piece. "We've been eating seafood." She dangled the gum in her face. Then she winked at Brooke and joined Philly in the room.

Brooke ran over to Royal's purse and dug through it. There it was, the blue serum, sitting right at the bottom. *This hot bitch wants to sleep with Philly. I got something for both they asses. Philly just don't know Royal only puts out, she don't give. And I give the best head known to woman and man. I'm gon' turn this mutha out. I'll fix that hot bitch.*

Philly immediately began to undress Royal, kissing her from head to toe.

Brooke hastily dropped her clothes and rushed over to them. She had the front, while Philly had the back. Brooke had the advantage because she knew exactly what Royal liked and didn't like. And she was pure lesbian, so she could please Philly with her eyes closed.

Philly turned on a Mint Condition greatest hits CD, as they lay on the floor in front of the burning fireplace.

Royal lay back on the plush, giant pillows as the women devoured her body.

At first, the two women fought like cats over a piece of meat, but after they found their favorite parts of Royal they simmered down and began their pleasure trip.

Philly lay on her back and directed Royal to sit on top of her face, facing forward, so she could eat her at the same time.

Royal made small kisses on Philly's thighs. She smelled so good, skin felt like butter. But once Royal got to her

juicy mound, she panicked and looked at Brooke helplessly.

Brooke laughed loudly. She knew it. It never failed.
Royal couldn't eat no pussy. So she crawled over, massag-
ing Philly's golden brown thighs, licking and sucking them
sensually. She tickled her clit with her nose, inhaling Philly's
sweet natural fragrance. Brooke was going to enjoy this
after all.

After two deep strokes of a flat tongue and a long, wet
suck, Philly pushed Royal up and looked down at Brooke.
She'd never had anyone eat her pussy like that before. It
felt better than an actual orgasm.

Philly changed their position. She wanted this night to
be all about Royal. She positioned Royal on her knees so
that she could perform her deadly act. She spread Royal's
big ass and dug in, sucking her asshole like there was no
tomorrow.

"Ummmm . . . ahhhh . . . yes." Royal rolled her ass on
Philly's mouth.

Brooke took this opportunity to make Philly hers. She
spread Philly's legs and slid her head between them, sucking and licking Philly's ass and pussy at the same time, ren-
dering her helpless.

Philly lost control and let go of Royal. "Damn, Brooke!
Shit!"

Philly reached around and pushed Brooke's head in
deeper.

"You like that thick, wet tongue." Brooke tried repeat-
edly to enter her pink insides, but it seemed like Philly's
pussyhole was closed.

Just as she was about to try again, Philly's body began
to jerk, and she opened up and skeeted like a water foun-
tain.

For the first time Brooke got a clear look at Philly's

pussy. "Ehhhhh, what the fuck is wrong wit' yo' pussy?" She released huge globs of spit onto the floor.

Philly became embarrassed and hurt. "Bitch, get outta my house!"

Royal looked on in confusion.

Brooke got up and grabbed her clothes. "Come on, Royal." She walked to the front and grabbed something out of her purse.

"I want you to stay. I got this." Philly picked up the brown pouch. "It's fifty thousand dollars in here. I'm going to give it to Brooke to leave you here with me. I'm not trying to buy you, just buy her off."

"No. I'd rather have her."

Brooke walked back into the room and helped Royal to her feet.

"I told you to leave my house." Philly lunged at Brooke and punched her in the chest, losing her balance and landing on the serum, which immediately took effect.

"Who's coming here tonight?" Royal placed the pink suitcase on the table and flipped it open.

"My New York partner. We're making a deal with the Haitians."

Brooke ran her hand over the drugs in the suitcase. "When and where?"

"After he picks up the dope and delivers it to them. We'll meet them at LaGuardia Airport and make the final exchange in two and a half weeks."

Royal told Brooke as they were gathering their things to leave, "We have to leave the drugs, but we can split the fifty thousand."

As they were on their way out the door, Brooke rushed back into the house. "Go ahead. I need to pee." She slowly walked up to the drowsy Philly.

"No wonder she stays with you. You eat pussy like a champ. I bet your pussy is just as good."

Brooke kneeled down beside Philly. "You could've been the one. You were perfect."

"She would have stayed if you left. She'll never love you."

"Yeah, and she'll never love you either." Brooke took the blade from her bra and slashed Philly's neck.

CHAPTER 47

As Wise pulled up the driveway, he could see that the front door of his house was cracked opened. He drew his gun and kicked the door wide open. "Anybody in here gon' get blown the fuck away."

He walked around and surveyed all the damage. The house had been turned upside down. The only room left intact was his daughter's. He sat down on her bed and rubbed his hand over his head. "What the fuck happened?" *Who would have done this shit? I don't have no known enemies. Could it be someone from the home team?*

Wise jumped up from the bed and ran to his safe. "Please be here." He opened the safe, and the key to his storage unit was gone. He changed his code every day, and since Pepper had been there, he shared the numbers to his fortune with only her. "Damn it!"

Ring, ring!

"Pepper!"

"Nooo, this is Tina. Pepper? What—"

He heard her sniffling, like she'd been crying. "What's wrong with my daughter?"

"She's in the hospital. And they said we have to pay for her treatment in advance this time." She began to cry harder. "This is the sickest she's ever been.

Wise hit the wall with full force, busting his knuckles. How could this bitch do this to him a second time?

"They have to do a procedure and it's going to cost three hundred thousand dollars. But she has to get two treatments a month for six months before the procedure."

"Don't worry 'bout it, Tina. Calm down. How much are the treatments?"

"Five thousand every month."

"I'll be there in about two hours."

He drove like a wild man to Buena Vista Road. Swerving the car into the U-Haul parking lot, he came to a screeching halt. He opened the large storage unit and it resembled his home—ransacked. All the makeshift furniture that was put there for a front was now overturned and cut up. Nothing was salvageable.

"Fuck me!" He picked up the pink, princess, pig bank that his mother had given his daughter and threw it to the floor. All the one thousand dollar bills scattered. This was all he had to his name ten thousand dollars.

He rushed back to the Medical Center and busted into Pepper's room, only to find an orderly putting fresh sheets on the bed, the IV machine gone. "Where's the girl that was in this room?"

"I don't know. I'm just cleaning the room for the new patient coming in now."

Wise hit the wall, and the orderly jumped.

"Did you see the person in this room leave or anybody come in or out?" His heart was in a knot and his breath felt like it was being cut in half. It was happening all over again. Damn it, what was he thinking?

"A group of girls came in and then they left. That's all I saw." The orderly backed away from the angry, young thug.

He had been set up. Pepper had got him in more ways than one this time.

Everyone in the minivan was quiet. Pepper was numb from head to toe as she held on to Ascada's hand.

"I know you loved him. I'm sorry."

"It was all for the best," Pepper said, trying to reason with herself. "He probably would have thought about what I did to him for Joc and turned on me anyway."

"He loved you, Pepper. I saw it in his eyes the night we were at the club and every day we spent with him."

They smiled at each other.

"I don't know how y'all pulled that one off," Royal said.

Ascada told her, "We had practiced it with cold water, so we knew exactly what had to be done."

"We had to get into a real argument and a real fight in order for it to look real. And when I saw they were doing a sleep study at the hospital, I knew. "

As they rode home, they discussed what was going to go down in New York in two weeks. They filled Royal, Pepper, and Ascada in on what was going on with Pig.

Kay, one of Pig's baby daddies, was knocked a couple of days ago. He was caught with the sandwich bag full of cocaine and two thousand dollars in cash that he took from Pig.

The detective banged on the table. "Son, who supplied you with the drugs?"

"What kind of deal are you going to give me?" Kay asked, trying to strike a deal to save his ass.

"You're going to do five years. Is that worth protecting someone who'll have another young person on the street tomorrow?" The detective flipped through the manila folder. "Look, give us the name of your connect, and we will make you a sweet deal." He adjusted the gun on his hip and sat on the edge of the table.

Kay couldn't tell on Pytra. She'd been the only person down for him through thick and thin. Maybe if he ratted out the other girls Pig told him about, then they could get all their money and dope and be on top.

"Moses, Spencer Mack's baby mama, some chicks name Amil, Royal, and Avada, Nescada, something like that."

Lately the detective and his partner had been hearing from their street informant that a clique of females were robbing connects and selling the stolen dope to local drug dealers. If this was the same group of females, then they would bust the Atlanta drug ring wide open.

CHAPTER 48

Dyson Humphries loosened up his tie as he walked swiftly to his 2007 SL Mercedes Benz. He surveyed the parking area to make sure no one was lurking nearby. If he knew what this case would entail, he would have forfeited all the money in the world.

After hearing that Robert Cantrell died, he received a brown envelope this morning explaining everything, from the fact that Judge Cantrell and Gabby Cantrell had set Spencer and his baby mothers up, to Gabby being Moses Whyte's mother and Gabby being the one to adopt Kemoni. And he was left looking like the one that had set everything in motion.

He drove fast to the airport, not taking any clothes or personal belongings except for his briefcase. Humphries was in such a rush, he didn't see the black minivan tailing him. He whipped into a parking space. He took pictures of all the papers from the envelope and pressed *send* on his phone.

"Hey, it's me. Take the boys and get to the airport. Your tickets are—"

"What's going on, Dyson? People have been calling the house all day."

"Don't question me, woman. Just do as I say."

Humphries opened his car door and bumped a woman passing by.

"You should watch who you run into," the sassy woman said.

"I'm in a hurry."

"So that means you have no respect for women?" She fumbled around in her purse.

"Fuck you! I got enough problems."

Just as he turned his back and leaned in his car to retrieve his briefcase, the woman shot him with a stun gun.

"Ahhhhh! You fuckin' bitch!"

She kneeled down beside him and stunned him again. "I really thought you were on my side, promising to help me do everything in your power to try and get Kemoni."

She reached inside his car and grabbed every piece of paper in sight and out of his briefcase.

"But you were all about the money, taking from both sides of the tracks. All you had to do was follow the plan and not get caught up in what those whores said." She snatched the sunglasses and brunette wig off. "You and Robert thought you were the only two playing games, trying to turn me in to the Supreme Court for punishing the bitch that I carried in my womb for nine months. Spare the rod, spoil the child." She tapped him on the forehead.

"You crazy bitch!" He was foaming at the mouth.

"Anyone that tried or tries to help that black bitch will pay with their life."

"You killed Robert. I knew you were no good the night you let me fuck you on my desk."

"By any means necessary, Dyson." She turned the volume up on the stun gun and electrocuted Dyson Humphries to death.

CHAPTER 49

For days Emil and Mo tried to contact Humphries, but to no avail. DFACS still wouldn't talk to them or let them see their children. His secretary gave them a note instructing them to leave the rest of the money with her and that he would be in touch.

"What are we going to do now? Humphries is out of town." Mo hit the office door.

"His secretary said that he should be back at the end of next week. That should give us enough time to take care of Pig, go to New York, and get back here to get the girls." Emil tried to convince herself that everything would be all right.

"Why do we need to do New York anyway?" Nevada asked, feeling uneasy about stepping back into her old stomping grounds.

"Because if you can live off of eight thousand dollars apiece and still get Spencer out, then please share your idea with me." Mo pushed past Nevada and walked out of the law office.

❖ ❖ ❖

All of the girls sat in the minivan and watched Pig's house like hawks. They saw two different men leave within the same hour and they knew the kids were inside.

"She is such a triflin' whore," Royal said.

"What whore you know ain't triflin'?" Mo looked at Nevada.

"What y'all plan on doing to this girl?" Koi asked, not wanting to get involved with no mess. She'd had enough bad luck in her life.

"Whatever's necessary."

They jumped out the van like a pack of hoodlums. When they knocked on the door, Kaja answered wearing nothing but a thin, dingy white T-shirt. The air inside the apartment had to be colder than the winter air outside.

"Oh, Mo and Emil." She ran to them and hugged them tight. "Please take me with you. I prayed last night that you would come and save me."

"Save you from what, sweety?" Mo ran her hand over Kaja's bushy, tangled hair.

She looked toward her mother's closed bedroom door. "Please just take me with you," she yelled loudly.

"Shhhh, honey. I promise we will see about that. We need to talk with your mom."

As they all scooted into the small, nasty, cold apartment, Koi noticed blood on the front of the little girl's T-shirt. She knew all too well what it was like to want to get away, but have no outlet.

When she was a small girl, her Korean mother allowed her deranged father to abuse her sexually. He would put a chain around her neck, make her get down on all fours, and pull her around like a hound and make her sniff out the enemy.

"Get in there and find them pinch-eyed devils," her father would yell, remembering his time serving in the Vietnam war. He only heard the battlefield.

"Daddy, please . . . my knees hurt." Koi's knees would split and bleed because he never gave them time to heal.

And, because of her Asian eyes, in the middle of the night he would bust into her room and capture her, throw her down the basement steps and not feed her for days. He would beat her with a hose pipe, leaving long, ugly scars all over her body.

One day when she went to school with the wounds oozing blood, her teacher called the police. They rescued Koi and sent her to live with Mekia's family. But she was already mentally disturbed. It was only a matter of time before she snapped completely.

This is why she overcompensated with makeup, tight clothes and slutty acts. And now looking at this small, underfed, innocent child with blood on the front of her T-shirt and running down her leg, it woke up all kind of emotions inside of her.

"Come on, little lady, let's get you cleaned up." Koi took her by the hand and led her to the bathroom.

Mo, Emil, Pepper, Royal, Ascada, and Nevada stood around Pig's bed, staring at her naked body. Her face was white as snow. A bag of coke and three full needles of heroin lay beside her.

Pepper kicked the bed. Pig made a movement, but did not wake up.

Mo slapped her in the face.

"What the—who? Kaja!" Pig yelled out, high and confused.

"No, stupid broad, guess again." Emil kicked the bed again. "Look at her leg. I'm not touching that hoe. She might be infected."

The deep wound on her thigh was oozing pus and clear fluid. Her skin was dry and ashy. And to their surprise, Pig didn't have in a colorful weave. She actually had long, silky, jet-black hair.

Mo yelled into her ear, "Pig, Pig, get cho nasty, triflin' ass up."

She jolted up from the bed and looked down at her naked body. She grabbed a night shirt from the floor and threw it on. "What are y'all doing in my room?"

"Who the fuck you been runnin' your mouth to?" Pepper asked her.

"I ain't told nobody nothin'." Pig attempted to leave the bedroom.

Mo snatched her back by her shirt, slanging her into an unstable chair. She jumped back up ready to fight with Mo but realized her room was full of women not on her side.

"You told your baby daddy everything that went down with us?"

"Kay don't know nothing. He just guessing."

"A detective came to mine and Emil house the other day asking questions about drugs, money, and Spencer's connects. You the only asshole I could think of that was full of shit enough to rat on us," Mo told her.

Pig didn't answer. She was plotting on how she was going to get to the gun or butcher knife in her top dresser drawer.

Emil was tired of the lies from everybody and all the games people were playing when it came to getting her child back. She kicked the chair over with Pig in it.

This time Pig jumped up and caught Emil with a left hook to her cheek.

Mo held Royal and Pepper back, because this was already an unfair fight.

Ascada noticed a brochure on the dresser with the word *AIDS* on it. She scooted over to the dresser as the two women fought like wild cats.

At first Pig was getting the better of Emil, scratching her neck and face up, but Emil bit a plug out of her arm and punched her in the stomach and she folded over. Emil kicked her in the face, and Pig fell to the floor, blood seeping out of the thigh wound and her mouth.

"Stop! Stop! She got AIDS! Full-blown AIDS!!!"

Koi walked in the room and left the door cracked. Kaja kneeled down by the door and peeped in to see what all the noise was coming from.

"What the fuck!" Emil slung the blood from her hand and jumped up off her. "Oh shit! Oh shit! I bit into her and drew blood." She ran to the bathroom, ignoring the little girl kneeling by the door and witnessing everything going on in her mother's room.

Mo grabbed one of the full heroin needles and stuck it into the open wound on Pig's thigh.

"What are you doing?" Royal asked.

"Overdosing this bitch. She don't mean nobody no good."

"What are we going to do about those kids?" Pepper asked.

Mo grabbed the other two needles and placed one in Nevada's hand and the other in Koi's hand.

Emil walked back into the room and knew immediately what Mo was doing.

During all the confusion, Kaja had quickly crawled under the bed. She was now witnessing all the madness and her mother's death, front row.

Koi pushed the needle back into Mo's hand. "I'm not getting involved with this mess."

Pepper told Koi, "You stole money, spent it, and you're here witnessing what's happening. Either way it goes, you're already involved."

Mo looked at Nevada without saying a word.

Nevada walked over and shot the heroin into Pig's arm, and Pig began frothing at the mouth.

Mo pushed Koi in the back. "Go ahead and finish it."

"No. No."

Emil walked up to Koi. "Your ass is out on the street if you don't do this. She ran her mouth, and who's to say you won't run yours. If you don't do this, you might as well lay down beside her." She grabbed the gun from Mo.

Koi began to cry. "Where? Where do I put it."

"In the other arm," Pepper told her.

Koi kneeled down beside Pig and stuck the needle in her arm.

"Push it," they all yelled.

When she pushed it into Pig's arm, her body began to convulse.

Kaja scooted from under the bed and tried to help her mom. "Mommy, Mommy," she cried, but Pepper grabbed her around the waist and took her into the living room.

Ascada stood motionless, flashing back to the day in Walsh when they made her do the same thing. She knew exactly what Koi was feeling and what her life was going to be like from this day forward being part of The Clique.

CHAPTER 50

It was December 30, 2006, the day of Pig's funeral, and The Clique was on their way to New York.

"Oh Lord Jesus! Help me, Lord! My only child! Oh the wicked devil has taken my Pytra." Pig's mother was more dramatic than the weave colors Pig used to wear in her hair.

"Come on, Ms. Short." An usher helped her down the aisle.

Mo, Emil, Pepper, Royal, Ascada, Nevada, and Koi sat anxious and nervous on the second row, thinking everyone in the room knew what they'd done. Kaja couldn't tell anyone what she'd seen because she was staying with Emil, and they kept her safer than the gold at Fort Knox.

When they rambled through Pig's room to make it look like a break-in, they found a diary she'd kept from the time she was nine. They confiscated it before they left her apartment that night. They knew every ungodly, awful thing that she had gone through and what made her the way she was.

The slick-haired, loud-suited, pinky-ring-wearing reverend wiped his greasy, sweaty face before he even spoke a word. "The Good Lord done took Sister Short's only child for the sake of the devil having his way with her."

Over the week preparing for the funeral, the clique stayed close as possible to Ms. Short, more out of guilt than making sure no one fingered them as the murderers, helping her with the obituary, getting the children situated with their fathers or someone fit to take them, and finding a suitable plot to bury Pig.

Her mother was still the same slick-talking, hustling, jezebel she always was, but now she hid in the shadows of the Lord.

"I sure thank y'all girls for helping me with all this," Ms. Short said as she sat down to write the obituary. "I didn't think Pytra had any friends, 'specially since she was on them drugs and thangs. I raised Pytra right. I don't know what caused her to spoil."

Pepper wanted to scream. Her mother would be saying the same bullshit and they were the ones causing their children to turn sour. "Well, Ms. Short, sometimes the people who the Lord put here to take care of us are the ones causing us the most damage."

Ms. Short cut her eyes at Pepper and fanned herself more rapidly. "Well, my nephew said that Pytra was supposed to have some money put up somewhere." She dapped her eyes, pretending to shed tears. "You girls don't know where she might have it, do you? I hope that heathen she had them chil'ren by ain't get it. This funeral is costing me all my money."

They already knew that her congregation had pulled together and took care of Pytra's funeral expenses and gave each of her children a thousand dollars apiece. But the guilt of killing her and her unborn child weighed heavy on all of them.

"Yes, ma'am." Emil stepped forward. "I don't know

about any money she had put up, but we collected ten thousand dollars for Pig, I mean Pytra, and we would like for you and the kids—"

"Whew! Thank you, Jesus." Ms. Short snatched the envelope so fast and hard out of Emil's hand that she fell back into one of the church pews. "Could you get that before the end of the day and get it in small bills? Them funeral folks wantin' they money."

As Mo surveyed the small group of people, she saw the neatly dressed detective that had come to her home questioning her about Pig and her involvement in the stolen drugs and money. He winked at her and mouthed the words, "I'll be seeing you real soon."

She did a double-take before turning back around. It couldn't be him. "I have to go."

"You can't go," Emil told her. "People will look at us suspicious."

"I said I—"

Just as Mo was getting up to leave, Kay, Pig's baby daddy, drunk and high, stepped into their row and pushed her back. "What did y'all do to her?"

Royal waved her hand. "Leave," she whispered. "Get outta here."

"What'd y'all bitches do to her?" he said a little bit louder. "I had just left her and she was fine." He began to cry.

"Look," Mo said, slightly touching his dirty sweatshirt, trying to push him back out the aisle, "we will help you any way we can. Come on, come with me."

He snatched away from Mo, stumbling, grabbing on to the pew, getting extremely loud. "You killed her!"

Everyone in the church turned in their direction.

Jovan's and Mo's eyes met, and Mo slid back down in her seat.

Kay reached over and grabbed her by her dress collar

and began to shake her violently. "Why did you kill her? What did—"

Jovan grabbed Kay from the back, as Emil and Pepper popped him in the face from the front.

The detectives ran over, pulled Kay outside, and had him arrested for assault, disorderly conduct, and public intoxication.

Jovan sat down on the pew beside Mo. "Why haven't you returned my calls?"

Mo kept her face straight ahead.

"Talk to me." He pulled her hand to his lips and kissed her on the palm.

Mo wanted to run out of the church, away from the mess she'd created with Pig, and from Jovan, a man who'd only wanted to love and take care of her.

"Where have you been? Why are you treating me like the bad person? I just want to love you." Jovan watched tears run down Mo's beautiful face.

Royal could feel Mo's pain. "Go and talk to him. You need it."

"I-I-I can't. We're in too deep now. I don't want to involve him."

"I got involved the day I met you. I knew the circumstances when I saw you in that courtroom. I can handle whatever it is. Just let me in."

Mo jumped up and ran out the church and into her truck, but Jovan was quick on her heels. "I love you, Mo. Always know that."

But he wasn't quick enough. She closed the door and sped off, away from Pig's murder, The Clique, and Jovan.

CHAPTER 51

Spencer tossed and turned in his small bunk bed. Things in the joint had been rough since Kay told the police that the women had been robbing Spencer's connects. Word spread like wild fire. He'd been in three fights and had to shank a nigga to stay alive.

What the fuck have Mo and them done? This was supposed to be simple and quick. Now my own home team done turned on me, and the outside niggas done put a price on my head. They done killed Philly, and from what I'm hearing, they killed Pig too. And it looks like they may have killed Dyson Humphries.

Mo ain't been answering her phone, and since I put my mom in hiding, I can't contact her. She don't need to go to New York. They may already be exposed there too. She don't need to do this hit to get the money to get me out. I'll bid that little time in here.

Spencer thought about his children, Kaylen, Kaja, Kendall, Kemoni, Kamerion, Kayla, King, and the newest addition, Klarke, who not even his mother knew about. She was four years old, and Spencer had just found out about her the day he was locked up. Her mother, Jill, was young and wild and didn't want to take care of the little girl anymore, so Spencer told her to take Klarke over to his sister's house, his sister by his father.

Just two days before Humphries was killed, he got Spencer's charges dropped, except for some previous ones that he had to serve six months for. That's why he wanted to get in touch with Mo to tell her that they didn't need to go to New York. He had a bad feeling in his gut about how New York was going to turn out.

CHAPTER 52

Pepper had excitement in her eyes. She pictured herself performing on top of Radio City Music Hall. "So this is the Big Apple?"

"Yep, this is it." Nevada dreaded this entire trip. Something just didn't feel right. She couldn't eat or sleep. And when she did sleep she had nightmares about Big D choking the life out of her.

"Okay, ladies, we are here for two reasons, to rob Big D, and to get the money from the Haitians. We're after the money, no drugs," Mo reminded them. "No shopping, old boyfriends, or career dreams are to be sought after on this trip. We don't have long here, and we don't know if Big D and his crew know about us, so we have to be very careful."

"Tonight we have to hit two different spots at the same time to hurry the process along. All we need you to do" — Mo looked at Nevada — "is direct us to the two clubs. Then you take the cab back to the hotel."

Nevada slowly nodded her head up and down. She had

plans of her own, once she showed them where the clubs Tribeca and Shout were.

Koi sat nervously fiddling with her hands. Since the overdose they caused Pig to have, she'd been going crazy, thinking she saw Pig standing behind her in mirrors, and jumping every time a doorbell rang, hoping it wasn't the police coming to take her to jail.

What if that little girl tells someone? she thought. *I'm so sorry! I'm so sorry! But did I do the right thing by Kaja? When I took her to the bathroom and cleaned her up, she told me some things that should have justified my actions in killing Pig.*

Kaja told Koi, "My brother's daddy made me put baby powder up my nose, and it burn real bad."

"Why did he do that, honey?"

"He said that it would make me relax and be happy. He said it would make me feel better down there." Kaja pointed to her bloody vagina.

Koi wanted to run out of the bathroom and relieve Kaja of her pain—Pig. "What did your mom say?" she asked, rinsing the blood-soaked rag in hot water.

"She put the powder up her nose and showed me how to do it."

"What happened when you told her it burned your nose?"

"She told me to swallow a handful of it."

"How did you get so bloody?"

Koi saw the pain on the little girl's face as she looked down toward the floor and played footsy with herself. She lifted her chin up. "You can tell me anything. I won't think you are a bad child." She hugged the bright-eyed child.

"He put his giant pee-pee in my mouth and my butt."

"He didn't put it in your 'tutu'?"

Kaja shook her head no. "He tore my butt."

"Bend over on the toilet and hold on tight, okay. It's going to burn pretty bad, but it will heal and make it feel a lot better." Koi doused the rag with what was left of the witch hazel, and placed the rag between Kaja's small butt cheeks.

She screamed out, "Ouchhhhh! Ahhhhh! Noooo!"

"I'm sorry, but I promise it will make it feel a lot better. I know first-hand." Koi blew Kaja's burning, torn butt. "Where was your mom when he did this to you?"

"Right there telling me—ouch, ouch, it burns!" She yelled, jumping up and down.

"Okay, okay." Koi blew some more and waved her hand like a fan, to help comfort the little girl.

"She told me to relax or it was gon' hurt even more. But I kept on screaming for him to stop. Then my mama covered my mouth, and he kept going until my butt split."

"Dumb bitch," Koi said to herself. She rubbed Vaseline on her raw bottom. "That should make it fe—"

"Nice lady, are you taking me with you?"

Koi looked into the helpless little girl's eyes and saw herself. She wanted to say yes and take Kaja with her, but what was a damaged adult going to do with a damaged child? Most damaged adults were selfish, self-absorbed, and mentally unstable. And this was true of Koi. She knew the trick for the torn butt because her father would stick a broom or anything he could find up her rectum to punish her.

"Sweet girl, I don't have anywhere to take you."

Kaja hugged Koi tightly around the neck. "Find one, please."

Was she justified in killing a woman who gave her eight-year-old daughter drugs, let a man rape her knowing she had AIDS and that sex with that same man could possibly infect her own daughter?

❖   ❖   ❖

Emil snapped her fingers. "Koi, Koi, are you with us?"

"Oh, yeah, yeah."

"So, last time . . . if we can't find Big D before midnight, then we leave and go straight to the airport to take the Haitians and we out."

CHAPTER 53

Once they were in their hotel suite, Mo made sure all eight of them had their guns, pepper spray, and the serum. They got dressed, said a prayer, and jumped in a cab and headed into the city nightlife.

Emil, Ascada, and Pepper stepped into Shouts and faded into a dark corner, letting their eyes search the room for Big D. He looked like a one-eyed, bald-headed, jagged-toothed gorilla. And for hours, no one fit the bill.

On the other side of the strip, looking like top-notch royalty, Mo, Royal, Brooke, and Koi slid through the doors of Tribeca.

Nevada sat in the cab and watched them enter the club. She wiped the tears from her eyes. "Good luck," she said aloud behind a closed window. She was very thankful to them for helping her, accepting them into their clique, especially after what she'd done in the beginning. "To the airport please." She sat back and blew a sigh of relief. She was going to get her daughter and leave Atlanta behind.

But what Nevada feared and was unaware of was that

Big D had seen the group of females get out of the cab and leave her behind.

Big D had heard about all the hits on the big connects and figured they'd be coming for him next. If he had stopped by Shouts first like he'd planned and gotten to Tribeca a little later he would have definitely been got.

Those were some of the finest pieces of ass he'd ever seen. And then, when he saw the beautiful, flawless, porcelain face that he'd taken care of for so many years sitting in the cab, he couldn't believe his eyes. She'd actually had the balls to come back home to his stomping grounds

Big D shot back to his car and got behind the cab and made a phone call. "Aye, you know those girls that they said been doing the connects, and killed Philly? I think I done spotted 'em, *G*. Do me a favor. Pick Layla up from Shouts, and I'll call you in 'bout an hour and let you know where to meet me."

"I got you," the husky, female voice replied. "I can't wait to get my hands on the bitches that killed Philly."

Since Layla had gotten to New York she'd been hot in the ass and fly at the mouth. On top of that, she was sneaking around seeing Big D's biggest rival, and he wasn't having the same shit happen twice. He would kill two chickenheads with one gun.

CHAPTER 54

Nevada exited the cab, and just as she dug in her purse for the cab fare a ruff voice from behind her said, "Here you go," and gave the cab driver a hundred-dollar tip.

She had already begun to cry. Her heart had dropped into the seat of her panties. She knew she shouldn't have come back to New York. It was just too good to be true.

He politely grabbed her hand and tried to direct her to his truck.

"Nooo, I got a plane to ca—"

He looked her dead in the eyes and squeezed her hand until it felt like her knuckles were being crushed into one. "Stay a while. Haven't seen you in a long time." He pulled back his shirt, revealing his gun. "Don't make a fuss. Just get in the damn car. If you don't, I'll waste your ass right here in the street." He slung her purse into the street and pushed her into his black Yukon.

As they drove away from the airport, he asked her a million questions, like a long-lost, lovesick lover. "So what happen, Nevada? Why you run out on me and stole my shit?"

She couldn't talk. Her mind was on never seeing her child again. She knew he was going to kill her.

Smack! Pop! He bashed her in the face with his fist. "Why did you leave me? What did I do to deserve you treating me like that, huh?"

Nevada spat a tooth into her hand. "Stupid."

"You were more than stupid. You wrote your own death sentence." He picked up his phone and called someone. "Tonk, bring that piece of trash up to the warehouse."

They rode until there was nothing but trees in sight. "So when you start robbin'?"

"My daughter got taken," Nevada said like a small child.

"So you had a baby when you pleaded with me not to have one? 'Cause you said you didn't think you could be a good mother." But he already knew that she'd had a child with Spencer.

He pulled into a wooded area with a big black-and-red warehouse. He slapped Nevada in the face again then told her, "Give me a kiss."

She did as she was told.

He smacked her again. "That wasn't good enough. Take yo' clothes off."

"What?"

He punched her in the stomach. "Bitch, get them clothes off!"

She quickly took all her clothes off.

"Now get out."

Just as he told her to get out, she saw headlights coming down the rocky driveway.

He walked up behind her and hugged her waist, kissing her on the neck.

Layla jumped out the car, dressed like a video star, and

rushed up to them. "What the fuck is going on? Bitch, get off my man!" But Tonk grabbed her before she could swing on Nevada.

"What's up, baby? Glad you could join us."

Layla looked suspiciously at the naked white girl and her bloody face. Something was wrong. "Are you high, Big D?"

"High off you two. The two women who fucked me raw, with no Vaseline. And, get this, for the same nigga at that. Y'all got more in common than y'all know."

Big D said into Nevada's ear, "I know you left here pregnant with that bitch Spencer baby. I give you an A for knowing to get the fuck away from me before I killed you and your bastard."

"What do you mean, a baby by Spencer?" Layla asked, getting an attitude.

"Ain't that bastard you got me taking care of Spencer's seed too?" Layla felt a sickening feeling forming in the pit of her stomach. She'd been seeing Big D since she was a month pregnant with Kayla. When she saw that Spencer made no effort to leave Mo, she made her move on him and told him that the baby she was carrying was his.

Layla remembered that Tonk had left the car running, so she played him until she could make a dash to the car. "She is yours, Big D. Kayla is ours." She took a few steps toward him and Nevada.

Big D shook his head, trying not to believe Layla. "I seen them money order receipts you sent to Spencer in jail, with my money." Big D frowned his face.

"Fuck Spencer! I love you," she screamed for effect.

"Y'all hoes don't love nobody but y'all self." He shot Nevada in both feet and slung her into the truck.

Nevada fell hard into the truck. "Ahhhhh!!! Oh God!" She hooked her arm into the open window to hold herself up.

"That's for running away from me. Now hold yo' hands up."

"Kill these hoes and let's get to the airport. It's eleven o'clock," Tonk said, aggravated by the whole soap opera drama.

"Tonk, both these hoes got some good snatch. Take one of 'em up in the warehouse, wear that ass out." He laughed, slapping his thigh. "Well, in yo' case, eat 'em or whatever you do."

"Fuck you, nigga. I'm as much man as you."

Layla took off running to the car and made it to the door, but Big D shot her in the back of both thighs, and she fell, hitting the jagged rocks.

He walked over to her. "You thought I was gon' let you get away from the grips of the beast?" He kicked her over onto her back, then in the ribs, cracking two of them.

"Please, please, baby, I—"

"Am a worthless piece of pussy, let me hear you say it!" Big D was jumping around like a crazy man. His adrenaline was in overdrive.

Layla was in excruciating pain, moaning and mumbling Big D's words.

But he couldn't hear her, so he kicked her again with the hard-leather Timberland boots. He stepped on her face, pressing his boot hard into her face, leaving the Timberland imprint on her face. "Speak, hoe! You always got something to say. Say it now!" He shot Layla in each of her hands. "That's for taking my money and spending it on another nigga!"

"Ahhhhhhh! Ohhhhhhh, noooooo!" Layla screamed out.

Nevada saw a gun sitting on the seat of the Yukon. She opened the car door and grabbed the gun. She was going home to her daughter. Fuck Big D, The Clique, and Spencer.

"You thought I wasn't gon' find out about yo' triflin' ass?" He shot her twice more, in the groin and the stomach. "I'ma kill both y'all hoes and leave y'all stankin' out here in the woods." He put the gun on top of the car and pissed in Layla's eyes and mouth.

Nevada jumped in the truck and took off, shooting out the window, hitting Big D in the face and the chest. She tapped Tonk with the driver's side mirror, and she fell to the ground.

Unharmed, Tonk jumped up and squeezed her shoulder. She checked Big D's pulse, and it was faint. But Layla wasn't so lucky. She was dead.

Tonk looked at her watch. Eleven forty-five. She had just enough time to get to the airport and make the deal with the Haitians herself. She grabbed the four-million-dollar suitcase, called anonymously for some help for Big D, and headed to the airport.

CHAPTER 55

Mo called Emil and the other girls. "It's been two hours. Let's go to the airport. We can't wait no more."

"I ain't seen no gorilla-looking nigga yet," Emil said without looking to see who was calling.

"We headed out. It's eleven-fifteen. Y'all catch a cab down here, and then we'll go from there."

"I tried calling Nevada at the hotel room, but she didn't answer. We'll just see you in a minute."

As they rode up to the airport, a black Yukon sped by them.

"I could have sworn that was Nevada in that truck," Koi said.

"Naw, she probably getting some much-needed rest," Pepper said.

They walked down to the parking garage and set up behind a huge green dumpster. They put on black ski masks and black lipstick.

Ascada was getting nervous. "What time is it?"

"Five minutes to twelve."

"Y'all sure y'all need me? I mean I can go back up—"

Emil jumped across Royal and started choking Ascada.

Royal grabbed Emil around the waist and threw her to the side. "Y'all, stop it. We got to—"

"Fuck this! I don't have to be here." Ascada pulled herself off the ground and started walking across the parking garage.

"Let that bitch go," Emil screamed. "She always fuckin' up shit anyway."

Just then, a black Yukon swerved into a parking space, a blue Range Rover did the same, and a champagne-colored Cadillac cruised through slowly.

Emil squatted back down behind the dumpster. The one vehicle they didn't see was a black Suburban parked two rows behind them.

"I got to go and get Ascada," Royal whispered.

They all heard her scream, "Ahhhhhhhh!"

They all jumped up with the masks and black lipstick on, and the champagne Cadillac came to a halt. They saw a car full of dreads and knew it was the car they'd been waiting for. The girls drew their guns and ran to the Cadillac. Mo and Brooke stood at the front of the car, while Emil and Koi took a side. Royal started walking in the direction Ascada did.

Pepper went to the back of the truck and shot the lock.

"Turn off the engine. Get out with your hands up. If you try and floor it out of here, we will shoot to kill," Mo said.

The three men in the car got out the car with their hands up. "What is this, man? Are you the chicks we suppose to be meeting? Now y'all gon' rob us?"

"Naw, *I* am."

They turned around and came face to face with their past.

She was dragging a pink suitcase, and Ascada by the hair like a caveman, her gun pointed at them.

"You might as well throw your gun down. You're out-numbered."

"Not while I have this bitch in my hands. Y'all won't risk her life."

Emil could see Pepper from where she was standing, but Tonk couldn't.

"Throw the guns down," Pepper mouthed. "I'll shoot her."

Emil winked at Mo. "Okay, you win."

They all threw their guns down.

"Which one of y'all hoes killed Philly?"

Royal was squatted down, creeping back around to where the Cadillac was parked. She was going to take her out. She aimed her gun and tried to shoot, but it was jammed.

Tonk studied their faces and saw that Brooke was the only one that didn't look confused by the question. "So it was you?" She walked up to Brooke and punched her dead in the face.

"You ain't forgot about that ass-whuppin' at Walsh, have you?" Mo bravely moved toward Tonk. "We can serve you up again if you need a refreshing."

Tonk raised her gun and prepared to shoot Mo in the head. "Bye, bitch."

Pow! A bullet came from somewhere in the garage and hit Tonk in the chest.

Then all hell broke loose. The three Haitians tried to reach for their guns, but gunfire met them in their chest, heads, and backs. The gunfire wasn't coming from Pepper, Royal, or Tonk, but from the black Suburban.

Ascada dropped to the ground, and crawled under the car, lying on her six-months-pregnant belly. She found out the day after she'd seen the AIDS brochure at Pig's house and needed to be checked after fucking Hunter's nasty ass. And when they ran a check for everything, she never thought she'd come up pregnant because she was still having her period.

Pepper's body froze up. She couldn't move because of who she saw coming toward them. The men rushed the Cadillac, shooting everything in sight.

As Brooke's riddled body fell across the car, Mo and Emil hit the ground, grabbing their guns from the ground, shooting back, and hitting two of the men.

Police sirens echoed through the garage.

"Shit! Just grab the girls," the leader screamed, dragging Ascada out by her legs, kicking and screaming.

One of the men ran back to help him.

"Take her."

He grabbed Ascada and took her back to the truck.

The leader looked in the car, around the car, and finally in the trunk. He saw a woman lying on the ground wearing a diamond *P* like the one he'd given to Pepper. He snatched the ski mask off and saw her face. Then he pointed his gun at her head, ready to unload, but he couldn't do it. He didn't know if she was already dead or not, but he picked her and the dope up and carried them to the truck, and cautiously drove past the speeding police cars.

CHAPTER 56

Ascada brought Royal a cool washcloth. "Maybe she in a coma."

"She ain't in no damn coma!" Royal yelled. "She still responsive. Her body is just in shock."

"I'm still trying to figure out what happened." Emil nervously bit her nails.

"Wisdom," Ascada said quietly.

The door to the hotel room opened and, Shilo, one of the men from the black Suburban, brought in bags of food. "It's some turkey sandwiches, chips, and sodas in here." He eyed Royal. "Anything else y'all need, let me know."

"Yeah, she need a doctor, and we want to go home." Royal stood up face to face with him.

Ever since he'd grabbed her at the parking garage and felt her soft body, smelled her sweet skin, and saw those crystal-clear eyes he was taken. He wished they'd met under different circumstances. "Well, miss lady," he said, "everybody just happen to be at the wrong place at the wrong time," and he walked out of their room.

"Fucker!"

Koi said, "Maybe if we make enough noise, someone will come up here and save us."

"Yep. Save our ass right to the jailhouse. Our fingerprints are on those guns we left behind, remember," Mo said. "Our best bet is to stay put for a while until we can think of a better plan."

"So what are we going to do with the bitches?" Domino asked. He was second in charge and a real woman-hating, hard-ass bully. He already knew exactly what he was going to do with Koi when Wise left to go see his baby.

"I don't know. Use them to rob some top dope boys." Wise rubbed his hand over his head. "I wanna know what happened to that pink suitcase. We all seen that butch carrying it and put it down."

"Man, it was so much gunfire in that place. Maybe it got slid under one of those cars." Shiloh was the level head of the group, the nice guy that thought before he reacted.

"I got to make it back down south before tomorrow," Wise said to his partners. "We need to set up some meetings to distribute these pounds."

Domino rubbed his hands together and grabbed his dick. "I got everything under control."

Wise went to the girls' room to see if Pepper had woken up. He wanted to slap the permanent taste out of her mouth and kill her when he saw her on the ground, but his heart wouldn't let go. "How she doin'?"

"Thanks to you, I don't know," Mo shot back.

"Can y'all go to the other room?" Wise asked nicely.

"Hell, naw! Why? So you can kill her for real?" Emil jumped in the bed and hugged Pepper.

The tall, powerful man came through the door, a gun in either hand. "Yo, Domino, take them to the other room."

Domino smiled, showing his full platinum grill. "Come on, bitches."

All the ladies, except Emil, got up. "I'm not leaving her."

Domino didn't ask her again. He grabbed her by the ankle and snatched her off the bed, causing her to hit her head on the floor.

"Ouchhhhhhh!"

He kept dragging her to the room, still holding her by the ankle.

Wise got in the bed behind Pepper and pulled her into his arms. He smelled her beautiful hair and kissed her on the neck. "Why do you persist on hurting and leaving me? You know how much I love you."

And he fell asleep with her in his arms.

CHAPTER 57

The little girl sat on the fluffy, chocolate, suede sofa. It was so fluffy, it looked like it was going to swallow her up. And that's exactly what she wanted to happen. To disappear from this crazy lady. As she continued to miss her mother dearly, her little heart was slowly losing its tenderness and innocence.

"There you are, darling. I thought you would be in your princess room watching cartoons." The woman sat the buttermilk pancakes, syrup, eggs, bacon, and chocolate milk on the table in front of the little girl. "Mommy made all your favorites."

The little girl's eyes lit up like light bulbs. "Mommy!" She took off running to the kitchen. Seconds later she returned with the same sad look on her face. "Where's my mommy?"

Gabby pulled the table closer to the sofa. "I'm your new mommy."

"You're not my mommy! My mommy is black!" Kemoni yelled into Gabby's face.

Gabby brutally slapped the young child across the face,

and Kemoni hit the floor, holding her face, screaming like a wounded animal.

"Shut up, you little ungrateful heifer!" She snatched Kemoni up by her shirt and slung her into the sofa. "That's what's wrong with y'all people. Don't know how to respect someone trying to help you."

Gabby grabbed her psychiatric medication and popped two of them. She was a diagnosed schizophrenic. And trying to convince this child that she was her mother was draining her.

She tossed her hair over her shoulder and gave Kemoni the biggest, sweetest smile. "Now eat your food for mama."

Kemoni was hungry, thirsty, and exhausted. She'd been crying for three days straight. But she didn't trust this crazy-ass woman claiming to be her mother. She stared into Gabby's eyes and sternly said, "No."

Gabby picked up a pancake with her hand and drenched it with syrup. She stuffed it into Kemoni's mouth, damn near choking her. "I give up. Maybe if I starve you, you will eat for me. You just don't know what I've done so that we could be together."

Kemoni looked at the crazy woman with lost eyes. She'd started to go into her own mind to escape everything that was happening to her. She just wanted to be back at home with her mother and father.

CHAPTER 58

Pepper jumped up out of her sleep and realized she was laying next to Wise.

He pulled his gun out from under his pillow. "What? What is it?"

Their eyes met. She looked bright and fresh like nothing had ever happened.

"Just wanted to make sure you were all right." Wise tried to jump up, but Pepper pulled him back to her and hugged him.

Domino was peeping through the crack in the door. He knew this nigga was soft, still catching feeling off some broad who had robbed him and left him hanging. Shoot that ho, put your foot on her throat, and bury her out back. That was his motto. And that was the kind of leader this team needed. Not some pussy that had a soft heart and too many issues.

Wise pushed Pepper off him and jumped out of the bed. "That shit is for the birds."

"I'm so sorry, Wise. I-I-I don't even know how to explain it."

"Save it for the next man."

Pepper jumped out the bed, still feeling woozy, almost falling. "Please hear me out."

He kept walking.

"I love you, Wisdom."

He paused for a second and then thought about all the money she took, and his daughter being put on hold for her treatment because of it. Then he walked out.

The girls ran back in and hugged Pepper. "Chick, we thought you were dead."

Pepper rubbed her head. "I did too." She looked over her body to see where she was shot. "I wasn't shot?"

"Nope. All hell broke loose. Bullets were coming from everywhere, a black Suburban pulled up, and we were here," Mo explained to her.

"Who shot Tonk?" Pepper asked.

"I thought you did," Emil said, puzzled.

"No, I froze up."

"Well," Mo said, "must have been Royal."

"My gun jammed," Royal told them.

"Koi?"

"No, my gun was on the ground, remember?"

"I'm just glad somebody did," Emil said. "You hungry, Pepper. You haven't eaten in three days."

"No, I'm not hungry." Pepper was confused. The single gunshot came from a direction other than where Wise and his boys came from. *Somebody else was in that parking garage.*

Mo turned on the television, and shock hit her body. The other girls surrounded the TV as well:

"No, Paul, the only information we have at this time is that it was a drug deal gone bad. Four are confirmed dead, and some women are missing. We are going live to our brother station in Atlanta, Georgia, with Jovan Mims. Jovan, go ahead."

"Thanks, Paul. What happened at LaGuardia Airport's park-

*ing garage has been a mystery since day one. The bags left behind
show evidence of at least four more Atlanta women. It's like they
disappeared into thin air. Where are they? They could be kidnapped
or possibly dead."*

Mo touched the screen. "I'm alive. I'm right here, baby."

"I'm Jovan Mims with CNN news."

Jovan had at least two more minutes of coverage, but he
spotted someone he desperately needed to speak with.
"Mrs. Cantrell!" He ran after her. He knew everything
there was to know about her and Mo. "Mrs. Cantrell!"

She walked faster the first time she heard him call her
name, but he sprinted and caught up with her.

"I'm not doing any more interviews until this case is
solved."

He couldn't believe this beautiful woman was the monster Mo had described to him. "Mrs. Cantrell, I just want
to let you know that I am doing everything in my power to
find Moses."

She laughed in his face, swinging her blonde hair to her
back. "She has gotten to you too? Boy, it must be in her
genes. Why are you telling me this?"

"Gabby, don't you want to find your daughter? Your
grandchild's mother?"

She looked around to make sure no one had heard him.
"Look, I don't' know what kind of game you're trying to
play, but believe me, if you play one with me you will lose.
That bitch ain't my daughter."

He stared into her dark blue eyes and saw nothing but
evil and hatred. "I'm sorry, Mrs. Cantrell. I had you mixed
up with someone else."

Gabby smiled like she'd never said anything wrong.
"You have a nice day, young man." And she walked away.

"Excuse me," a light voice said.

He turned around and came face to face with a battered-faced young woman. He knew he'd seen her somewhere before, but he couldn't put his finger on it.

She was holding her hand over her mouth as she talked. "You don't know me, but I know the girls you runnin' the story on."

Jovan took out a pad and pen. "What's your name? And I will contact you."

"No, I don't want to go on record." She pulled him by his jacket arm over to a concrete sidewall and leaned up against it. "I know you love Moses, and you should. She's a good person despite how the latest events in her life have made her act. I just wish we could've met under different circumstances."

Jovan turned off his media mind and focused on finding Mo. "What kind of circumstances did y'all meet under?"

She dropped her hand from her mouth and looked toward the ground, resting her hands on her knees. "Lies, betrayal, men, money, drugs, murder, you name it." She looked up into the bright sun, squinting her eyes and lips up.

For the first time, Jovan saw why she was hiding her mouth. She was missing her front tooth. He reached into his pocket and pulled out his business card, scratching through his business number, writing in his cell and home number. "Here, call me if Moses contacts you or you hear anything. I want Moses to come home safe to me and her daughter."

"After everything that's happened, I hope she does too."

"I have interviews with some of the family members of the missing women. I hope you will join us. It's Wednesday night, and it's going to be live."

She closed-mouth smiled at him and squeezed his hand before walking away.

Images from the courthouse and the church flashed in Jovan's head. In court, the day Cantrell was acting a fool, he'd written down the names of Spencer's baby mothers.

Now he remembered where he'd seen her before. He stood up and yelled, "Nevada!"

CHAPTER 59

"Nevada!" Pepper yelled out. "That's who shot Tonk." She rubbed her neck. "And she stuck me in the neck with a needle."

"She's the one who saved me?" Mo asked, not wanting it to be Nevada who was responsible for saving her life.

Royal got up. "That's why you were out so long. She shot you with that last batch of serum I made. It was double the dosage."

"Her face was bloody. She looked wild, like she had been fighting." Pepper shook her head back and forth, trying to remember everything that took place. "Come to think about it, she only had on a shirt that came to her thighs and no shoes. And her feet were bloody."

"Her feet?" Mo asked.

"Yeah, both feet."

Royal went to the bathroom and got a cool rag. "Maybe you need a little more rest." She folded the washcloth and placed it on Pepper's forehead.

Pepper slapped the washcloth away from her face. "I'm

for real. We have to find Nevada. She must be the one that took the money."

Bam!

Domino bust through the door. "Which one of y'all hoes givin' up the pussy tonight?"

None of them answered. They just looked at him like he was crazy.

He pulled out his gun and cocked it. "I said which one of y'all givin' up the pussy?" He already knew that he was taking Koi. He just wanted to put fear in their hearts to keep them in fear of him.

None of them still gave him an answer.

He walked over to Ascada and fondled her full breast. She hit his hand away, and he retaliated by slapping her face. "Don't you ever touch a pimp." He stroked his already hard dick and walked up on Koi.

"I'm on my cycle." She gave him a cute smile.

He laughed like Jolly Saint Nick. "Let me see."

She looked big-eyed at him, dropping her smile. "I-I-I—"

He put the cold steel to her head. "I said let me see."

"How?"

"Drop them drawers, open up yo' legs, and spread yo' pussy lips."

She sat back in the chair and did as he told her to do, exposing a pink pussy, minus the red.

The other women turned their heads, while Domino licked his hungry lips. Her pussy looked sweet and meaty. "Jus' like I thought." He snatched her up by her throat.

Pepper ran to Koi's defense. She figured since he knew she was sick he'd have some compassion for her. "Look, she's already . . . we've already been through enough. Just please let her—"

Domino pimp-slapped Pepper to the floor.

The other women stood up to jump him, but he quickly

pulled out another gun to join the one he already held. "I'll either kill or maim y'all asses before you come close to me."

When he knew he had control again, he put one gun up and took Koi to the other room.

Koi stood in the middle of the floor like a nervous child. Her mind was racing a mile a minute trying to figure out a way to get outta there. "What do you want me to do?"

"Everything." Domino dropped his pants to the floor and grabbed his dick, stroking it with major force. "I like it rough and hard. Get over here on yo' knees."

As soon as Koi got within his reach, he shoved his dick down her throat.

Koi hesitated. Even though she was the biggest slut in hip-hop, she always made men wear condoms when she was giving head or sitting on their laps.

He slapped the back of her head. "Get wit' it."

She wrapped her wet lips around his dick and applied pressure.

"Yeah, that's what I'm talkin' 'bout."

After thirty minutes of her sucking and deep-throating him, she said, "My jaws hurt." *This crooked-ass dick probably don't work right anyway. Muthafucka got me sitting here blowing for almost an hour on a malfunctioned dick. If I could reach that gun I would blow his damn brains out.*

He pushed Koi onto the floor and stood over her. "What the fuck you tryin' to say? Something wrong wit' my dick?"

"I jus' said my jaws hurt."

"I'll show you what hurt jaws feel like." He punched her like he was fighting a man.

She dodged the most severe blows, but the ones that caught her in the jaw were painful.

After he beat her until he was tired, he sent her back to the other room.

CHAPTER 60

Shiloh came back two days before Wise. He had an itch he wanted to scratch. His curiosity about Royal was getting the better of him. Something in her face, her eyes, her mannerisms was familiar.

He took them all steak, potato, and salad dinners.

Royal watched him the entire time he was in the room. He was so sexy, strong, and sweet. She wanted to get to know him better.

"Thanks a lot for the good food. We didn't even eat anything yesterday. Ol' mean ass forgot about us," Royal told Shiloh as she pinched off a piece of a dinner roll.

He flashed his perfect white teeth. "You welcome, beautiful. And you say that Domino didn't feed y'all yesterday?"

"No, and the other days he brought in peanut butter, jelly, bread, and water."

"I apologize 'bout that slum nigga. He got women issues. Let me know if you need anything else."

Just as he was about to walk out the door, Royal touched his shoulder. "I hope you don't have to leave us anymore. Domino is a real asshole. He raped and beat up Koi."

Shiloh searched the room for a damaged face. His eyes landed on Koi. The left side of her face was bruised and swollen. "Hey, shawty, with the swollen face," he called out to Koi, "Domino did that to you?"

"Yes," Koi answered.

"Jus' please don't leave us again. He told me if he couldn't get what he wanted out of Koi then he would get it out of me," Royal said, hoping that he would have some type of compassion.

"I promise, if I have to go anywhere I'll be sure to take you with me."

Shiloh walked back into the room with Domino. "How'd it go with the women?"

"Mannn, I done told you them is bitches and hoes. Women don't exist no more."

"Well, you sho' can't beat 'em like slaves either."

"What I do on my time is my business. Don't forget who in charge."

"Don't let that in-charge shit go to yo' head. The only reason you got any clout is because you knew them Haitians were gon' be carrying weight."

Domino waved Shiloh off. "Nigga, I seen how you look at that big-booty, Amazon-lookin' bitch with the gray eyes. You and that nigga Wise gon' learn to treat these hoes like hoes. And me knowing bitches the way I do, that little slim bitch pregnant. You might wanna check on that while they runnin' to tell my business." And with that, he walked out the door.

CHAPTER 61

Spencer left the TV room with a blank stare on his face. The news reporter said that usually after a month of someone missing the police would turn it over to homicide. And it'd now been a month and a half.

He punched the wall. "Damn it!" No one on the streets had a lead or any information on where Mo and her girls could be.

The deal with the Haitians was their idea, so he didn't know anything about it. He would have told them not to even try it. The situation was too dangerous, and you never knew who was going to be on the other side.

Chuck assured him that he was going to make a deal with a new connect in a week and once he made twice the money back, he would find a new lawyer and hopefully get him out within the month.

As Spencer walked down the dark hallway to the kitchen, a tall, dark figure was approaching him. He moved over, giving the man more than enough space for them to walk down the narrow hallway. But the man still managed to bump Spencer's shoulder.

" 'Cuse you, homeboy," Spencer said, not turning around.

"Naw, 'cuse you." Kay stuck the shank deep into Spencer's back, side, then his back again, and Spencer fell to the floor, trying to catch his breath.

"That was for Pig, from hell, and for your baby mama killing her. See you in hell. Then he slit his own throat.

The guards rushed to apprehend Kay and take Spencer to the hospital.

CHAPTER 62

The community center was packed to the brim with family members, children, false witnesses, and CNN cameras and crew. Jovan looked around the room at all the characters who wanted to be famous, put their faces on TV at the expense of another human being's life. Then his eyes landed on one face that he knew was the truth.

"What's going on? How you been?"

Mekia's eyes were bloodshot red, and he was walking with a cane. His kids and a little girl named Jovan that he hadn't seen before, who resembled Kemion and Kaylen, were clutching to his waist and leg.

"Just trying to make it," he said with tears in his eyes.

"Anything I can do just let me know."

"Doing these interviews and getting the word out to the world is more than enough."

"Listen up, everybody. Helloooooo." Jovan had to stand on top of the table. "Shut the hell up!"

Everyone turned their attention to him.

"Thank you for coming out. My assistant Kay will take your name, number, and any information you may have if you are not family. If you are family, we will start the interviews now with Ascada's mother."

Mo, Emil, Pepper, Royal, Ascada, and Koi watched the TV like zombies. Ascada cried as her mother pleaded with whoever took her to let her come home. Hunter stood silent by her mother during the interview.

"We will pay any amount for her. Her husband and father want the kidnappers to know that we will not press charges. Just let her come home."

Next was Mekia and the kids. "Come home, mommy!"

Emil ran her fingers along the screen, tracing her children's face. She broke down even more when she realized Kaylen wasn't there.

"I want Emil to know that I still love her just as much as the day we got married. No matter what has happened, I just want you to come home. I love you." Mekia broke down as he hugged their children.

Emil realized she'd been a fool all these years for cheating on him.

Pepper sat straight up in her seat when she saw who was there pleading for her safe return.

Wise walked in the room without them knowing. He wanted to give her a chance to explain why she stole from him and let him know how it had messed up his life.

"I want Pepper to know that we are praying for her safe return. I love you so much, baby. I know you haven't heard mama say that in a long time, but I know you are alive and coming home to me." She moved aside.

Joc stepped up. "My love, how sorry I am for not being here for you. Whoever has her, I will pay any amount for her. Get in contact with Jovan Mims and he will give you the details. Pepper, I'm looking for you every day."

Pepper jumped out her chair and yelled at the television, "No fucking way! He is full of shit."

"Pepper, maybe he's telling the truth." Emil wiped her face.

"Yeah. 'Cause he thinks I'm dead."

"You just lovin' that other nigga again," Royal said.

"I've never stopped loving Wise," Pepper said with a serious, heartfelt tone. "I made a big mistake back then." She sat back down in the chair and held her throbbing head.

"Mommy, this is your King."

They all turned their attention back to television.

"Come home and get me, Mommy." He blew her a kiss.

Royal grabbed her chest and ran to the bathroom.

"Mommy? What the fuck?" Mo asked in disbelief. *How could Royal hide something like this from me? I'm her best friend. What the fuck is going on?*

"Moses Whyte, I'm doing everything I can to find out what happened to you. No matter what happened or happens, I'm always here for you." Jovan looked into the camera like he was looking into Mo's eyes.

Koi lay on the floor and began to cry like a baby.

"What's wrong, Koi?" Ascada asked, rubbing her back. Her and Koi had gotten close when they were in Columbus, Georgia.

"No . . . nobody was pleading for me to come home." Koi's spirit was broken. She felt like a nobody.

"Oh, honey, I'm sorry." Ascada helped Koi off the floor and wiped the tears from her face. "But just because there is someone there doesn't mean it's a good thing. Remember me telling you about Hunter."

Koi nodded yes and took a deep breath. "I damn sho' wouldn't want him waiting for me."

Ascada smiled at Koi, hoping to help ease her heartache.

Just as everyone was leaving, Kaja ran up to Jovan. "Mister, can you please get Ms. Mo and Ms. Emil home. I need a mommy."

"What's your name?"

"Kaja."

"Who is your mother?"

"Her name was Pig. Pytra Short."

Jovan kneeled down to Kaja's level. "You said *was*?"

"Ms. Mo and Ms. Emil killed her because she was a bad, bad mama. The other lady who helped me in the bathroom, she had a big ol' butt and had a lot of make-up on like a clown. She cried when she stuck the needle in my mama arm. The white lady did too."

Jovan took out a twenty-dollar bill and held it up to Kaja. "If I give you this, you got to promise to never speak of that or say that to anyone else. Promise?"

She smiled a big Kool-Aid grin. "Promise."

He handed the twenty-dollar bill to her.

Pepper heard the door click behind them. She saw the back of Wise's head going out the door. She tipped away from her emotional crew and went after him. "Wise."

He stopped in his tracks. He knew that sweet voice like the back of his hand. He answered without turning around to face her. "Yeah."

"We need some underwear, toothbrushes, and some other feminine products."

"Spend some of that money you stole from me." He started to walk off.

Pepper grabbed him by the shoulder. "Please . . . we need to talk."

Wise snatched away from her. "Ain't nothin' to talk about. You triflin' as hell and I fell for it again." He continued walking into his room, with her fast on his heels.

"I'm sorry!" Pepper screamed through heavy tears. "I was in a bad position." She threw her hands up in the air. "I can give you some of the money back."

He waved her off as he sat down in the chair. "Keep that shit."

Pepper paced back and forth. She wanted Wise to know that she didn't want to rob him, that it was all because of circumstances. "Me and Joc broke up, and I was broke as hell. Mo and Emil's children got taken when Spencer got locked up. Royal owed the government, and Ascada's gay husband"—Pepper just stopped herself. She didn't even know how to explain everything that went down in the past few months.

"Gay?" he asked, his lips turned up.

"Yeah, and we needed money bad. So we decided to rob Spencer's connects. You happen to be on the list as *CT*. I didn't know it was you."

"Man, save that shit for somebody who care. You could have pulled out when you found out it was me."

"I tried." She cried. "My back was against the wall and my feelings got caught up."

Wise jumped up like a wild man and backed Pepper into the wall. Breathing heavy into her face, he said, "Well, while yo' feelings were getting caught up, my daughter lay in a hospital dying." He clenched his jaws at the thought of his baby girl suffering because of his carelessness with this bitch. "The money you stole was for her treatments."

Once he realized that he was smashing her into the wall, he backed off and sat back down in the chair.

Pepper slid down the wall to the floor, holding her hand over her mouth. "Wise, I'm so sorry."

Domino was spying and eavesdropping around the corner. *This soft-ass nigga gon' fuck shit up with this broad on his heart. I'm gon' have to take these bitches out.*

"You're right. You are sorry. Sorry excuse for a woman." He was mad as hell at himself. How could he let her fuck up his world twice, jeopardize his daughter's life? He was ready to make everything right for them and would have given Pepper the money she needed.

Pepper crawled over to him and placed her hands on his

knees. "Please, Wise . . . I love you." She laid her wet face down on his lap. "I want to be with you. It's always been you."

"Look, why don't y'all just go on home. I saw the news." Remembering the sight of Joc, he forcefully pushed Pepper's head off his thighs. "You got people waiting on you," he said, mad as hell that he was reliving the same nightmare.

"We got just as much blood on our hands as you do." Pepper swallowed the thick lump stuck in her throat. "And nobody's waiting on me. My mama just need some money, and Joc is the one putting it in her pocket."

Wise shook his head. "Some shit never change, does it?" He stared into Pepper's eyes with disgust.

"I didn't—"

"Shiloh should be back later on today, and he'll take one of y'all out to get your stuff." Wise didn't want to hear her lame excuses. He wasn't going to be caught up in her shit again. "We have to keep a low profile. I'll be leaving tonight one more time, to make a quick deal and shoot the money to the hospital."

"Take me with you," Pepper begged. "Domino is a real bastard. I don't feel safe being alone with him." She really didn't want to be left alone with Domino, but she also knew this was a sure-fire way to be close to Wise. No matter how mad he was with her, he wouldn't let anyone harm her

Wise scooted to the edge of his chair. "He did something to you?"

"Just don't leave me," Pepper pleaded, throwing her arms around his neck.

CHAPTER 63

Shiloh and Royal went to Fred's and bought everything the women needed. Clothes, underwear, toiletries, and snacks.

"Thank you, Shiloh," Royal told him, showing all thirty-two teeth. "We really appreciate it."

"Bet. Y'all straight." *Ahhh, mann, what I would do with this dime-piece on my team. She's everything I've ever wanted in a woman.*

"I have to go out of town with Wise tonight, then to see my dad. I think you need to come with me."

She answered with no hesitation, "Okay."

"I been meanin' to ask you, Is one of your girls carrying?"

"Carrying?" Royal smiled. "Carrying what?"

Shiloh outlined a pregnant belly. "A child?"

Royal laughed, knowing that none of her clique was pregnant. "Nooooo. Why you ask that?"

"Never mind then. My mind be playin' tricks on me sometimes."

* * *

On the flight from Las Vegas to Florida, Pepper lay her head on Wise's shoulder.

He wanted to push her head into the window, but his situation was already stressed enough. He didn't need any more bad luck.

In the meanwhile, Shiloh and Royal sat across from them carrying on like a newlywed couple.

Shiloh told Royal that he started robbing because his father had AIDS, no insurance, and the medicine was expensive as hell. His mother died when he was nine and he didn't have any brothers or sisters. He was raised to respect women and take care of family.

Royal was excited to meet the man that had raised such a handsome, wonderful, young man. Was it really *robbing*, since he was taking from dope men?

CHAPTER 64

Domino led Koi into the dark room. "This time I'm gon' kill yo' ass if you don't perform like I tell you to."

While Mo and Ascada slept, Domino stole Koi right from beside them, like a thief in the night.

Koi just nodded her head. She was tired, worn-out on life. She had no hope of things getting better for her. Her mother didn't even plead for her to come home. And how could Mekia not even mention her name? She was numb. Nothing he could do to her would matter.

"Get that big, juicy ass up on that bed and spread 'em." She disrobed and crawled on the bed.

"Ahhh, no fight this time. So you do understand that I'm the pimp and you the hoe?"

"Yes," Koi responded, a disoriented look on her face, not knowing what was to come next.

Domino placed his gun on the bed beside them then parted Koi's big ass cheeks and rammed his raw dick into her ass.

As she screamed out in pain, he continued to dig deeper.

He didn't know that he was ripping old wounds in her ass, and her mind. Koi's anus had to be sewn up after her father went wild on her with a sharp knife.

"Damn, this ass tight. Shit!" He slapped her ass hard and watched it jiggle like Jell-O.

Without lubrication, her ass was rejecting his crooked penis, but that didn't stop him. He could feel her skin tearing, but the demon inside of him wouldn't let him stop. He rammed into her time after time, blood squirting out in the process.

The pain had numbed Koi's ass, but it couldn't numb her heart and soul. The force from him banging into her ass pushed her closer to the nightstand where Domino had placed his gun. She reached out and grabbed it.

BANG!

CHAPTER 65

Shiloh and Royal walked up to a four-story brownstone in Harlem. She was in a daze, staring at the wrought iron and marble staircase sitting in the middle of beautifully designed landscaping.

Shiloh smiled as he pulled Royal by the hand. "Come on." He told her to have a seat as he went in to get his father.

Royal looked in awe at all the hand-carved figurines, snow globes, and silver artifacts sitting on the fireplace, mantel, and side tables. She traced her finger over an elegant, silver picture frame that held a picture of the little boy in a sailor's suit. He looked to be the same age as King. *Mommy misses you, big boy. I'll be home to you soon. Stay strong for mommy.*

"He sleepin' right now." Shiloh paused as he entered the room. He saw her looking distant, touching the silver picture. "You know that handsome young fellow?"

She smiled to herself. "This handsome young fellow has to be you."

"Yep," he said, remembering the day he wore the blue-and-white sailor suit. He was eight years old, and it was his first time ever going to a fair. "You all right?" He gently rubbed the small of her back.

Royal shook off the thoughts of her son. She needed to stay focused so she could get home to him. "You said your dad was sleeping. That's fine. I'll meet him tomorrow. I'm tired myself."

Shiloh showed her to the guestroom. "If you need something, I'm right across the hall."

After hours of tossing and turning, Royal walked across the hall to Shiloh's room. She knocked softly, but didn't hear a response, so she walked on in.

He already knew she would come. He could feel her uneasiness when they first got there.

He accepted her with open arms. Neither one of them said a word as their bodies took control.

Royal sat her lusting, wet cave on top of Shiloh's full shaft.

"Umm, sssss," they both said as they squeezed each other.

She slowly moved her hips back and forth and side to side until she was dripping down his hips.

Shiloh slapped her big ass. "Work that shit."

Meeting Royal had to be God. He hadn't been in a relationship for at least nine months. His focus was on getting money for his father's medicine. No one had ever caught his eye like she did. And the best thing yet was that she had been single since six months after the birth of her child.

"Ooh, Shi." She pressed her fingers into his chest as she slapped her thick, juicy ass up and down on his pulsating dick.

"Yeah, baby, grab that dick. Make it cum."

"I'm 'bout . . . to—" Shiloh sat up, grabbed her around the waist with one hand, a handful of ass in the other, and pressed Royal's ass into him as he lifted up into her, and they exploded together.

Royal awoke the next morning to the smell of turkey bacon, cheese, eggs, pancakes, and fresh squeezed orange juice. She threw on the robe he had thrown across the bed.

"If you start something," she said as she kissed the back of his tan neck, "you better be prepared to continue it." She was in love already. So many men had tried her since Spencer, but there was something missing with each of them. But, with Shiloh, it jumped on her the minute he took her from the parking garage.

"I'm always prepared." He hugged and kissed her just as his father wheeled himself into the kitchen.

Joe cleared his throat. "Um, mmm."

"What up, Pops." He let go of Royal and went to push his father up to the table.

Joe couldn't take his eyes off Royal. She looked just like his first love.

For thirty minutes of conversation between Shiloh and Royal, he just stared at Royal, only saying an occasional, "Yeah," and "Mm-hmmm."

"Pops, the food ain't hittin' this morning? I cooked all your favorites."

"It ain't the food."

Royal looked at the man eye to eye.

"Where you from, girl?"

"Atlanta. Newbie, a small town outside of Atlanta."

"What's your mama name?"

"She's dead. She died when I was—"

"I said, what is her name?" he asked roughly.

"I think it's time for your meds." Shiloh pushed his father back to his room and gave him some medicine.

"I don't need no medicine. I know what I see. It's like seeing a ghost in my house."

Shiloh stuck his father with a Valium needle and he was out.

CHAPTER 66

"Oh shit!" Domino fell out of Koi's wet, bloody, ripped ass. "Oh shit, oh shit!" He reached out to touch her then snatched his hand back. He closed his eyes and shook his head to see if he was dreaming. but it wasn't a dream. It was live and in living color. Koi lay across the bed, the back of her head blown off.

For the first hour after she'd shot herself, her body involuntarily jerked.

Ascada and Mo ran through the adjoining door. They both covered their mouth as they looked at the scattered brain matter on the bed, walls, and floor. Then they looked at Domino.

"What did you do?"

"That crazy bitch, she-I didn't do nothing." He jumped off the bed and pointed the gun at them. "Get the fuck outta here! Get the fuck out!"

Ascada ran around hysterically. "We have to go to the police."

"Are you serious? We will go to jail. Koi's murder might as well be on our hands too."

"I'm not going back to jail. I just want to go home. Maybe the police will listen to us," Ascada said as she nervously bit her nails.

Mo and Emil felt like they were seventeen years old again.

"Ascada, listen to me, I want my child back. I don't want to go to jail again. Our prints are on those guns at the airport along with—"

"I don't give a shit, Mo! I have my own child to think about."

"What?" Emil and Mo asked shocked.

"I'm six months pregnant," she said, holding her stomach.

They looked at her stomach. It had a small pouch. "Why didn't you tell us?"

"I just found out when Pig died."

They embraced each other.

"Just calm down. Pepper and Royal should back in the morning. Then we'll all decide what to do together."

Just then, Domino came in the room after eavesdropping, only hearing that Ascada wanted to call the police. He twisted the silencer on the gun and fired a shot into Ascada's arm, and then another into her side.

"Nooooo! She's pregnant!"

When Ascada hit the floor with a thud, Mo and Emil rushed to her side and applied pressure to the wounds.

CHAPTER 67

Gabby sat behind her big new mahogany desk and laughed like a mad woman. She had everything she ever wanted. The last thing left on her to-do list was to make sure Mo was dead.

When they called to inform her that they had found a black, light-skinned Atlanta female dead at the crime scene of the LaGuardia Airport, she prayed and hoped it was Mo. It would save her the time and resources to do it herself. But when the forensics and fingerprints identified her as Brooke Jones, she knew her hunt was still on.

Bam, bam, bam! A hard knock on the door jolted her out of her trance.

"Come in." She watched in disgust as the greasy, slick-haired man slowly approached her desk.

"Here's the information you requested. They're in Las Vegas, staying in a rented cottage." The greasy man slung the envelope onto her desk and tried to sit down.

"No! Don't you dare sit down! My leather will not support that much filth and oil."

He laughed her off and leaned against the wall. "I see you makin' yourself at home in Rob's old seat." He picked the black smut from beneath his nail, popping it onto her precious leather chair. "Don't get too comfortable. It's always someone lurkin' around the corner, waitin' to take you out."

"What?"

He grinned at her. "Take your place."

Tossing her blonde, shoulder-length hair over her shoulder, she smugly said, "On my death bed."

The man coughed. "Soon."

Gabby gently opened her desk drawer, ready to retrieve her gun. She knew the greasy man was a stone-cold killer and wouldn't hesitate killing her in a heartbeat. "Excuse me?" she asked sternly, trying to show no fear.

Now that he had her attention, he continued. "The girls weren't kidnapped. They're hiding out with the men who took them. The men did take them, but when they figured they were in just as much trouble, they decided to stay on their own."

"Great. I'll pay them a visit." She got right on the phone and booked herself the next flight out, which was in two hours.

"And you are still here because . . ."

His patience was wearing thin with the overzealous, crooked D.A. He leaned over Gabby's desk and slammed his huge fist down onto her new mahogany desk, causing picture frames to fall and paperwork to fly. "My gotdamn money," he said in a slow, deep, gruff voice. "You shouldn't be such a nasty bitch. You never know who has your best interest in their hands." He brought his huge fist up to her nose.

Chills ran down her spine. She'd never felt as shaken or

scared in her life. She quickly slid the ten grand across the table.

"Spending Rob's money well, I see." He snatched up the money and walked out the door whistling "Take Me Back to Dear Ol' Dixie."

CHAPTER 68

After making the transaction in Florida, taking care of personal business in Harlem and Columbus, Wise, Pepper, Royal, and Shiloh all met back at the airport in Las Vegas. They rode in silence to the cottage, thinking about their last few days and the decisions that needed to be made.

As soon as they opened the door, Mo and Emil ran to them like hungry puppies.

"Royal, Ascada's been shot."

"What? Who did it?" Wise and Shiloh asked at the same time as they drew their guns.

Royal pushed past them. "Why didn't y'all take her to the hospital?"

"Someone might have recognized us. I don't want to go back to jail," Mo told her. "We didn't think it was that bad. We wanted to wait for you."

Royal rushed to the bed where Ascada was laying, panting and heaving heavily, and saying, "I need to push."

"You need to push what?"

Their eyes met.

"I'm pregnant."

Royal looked back at Shiloh to say, "Why?

"Okay, okay, calm down," she said, talking more to herself than to Ascada.

"Go get some hot water and as many rags you can find." Royal threw the cover back and saw that Ascada was bleeding profusely from the gunshot wound on her right side and from her vagina.

"Where's Domino?" Wise asked.

"That bastard did this!" Emil shouted.

Wise and Shiloh cocked their guns and knocked on the door. When no one answered, they kicked the door in and saw Koi's dead body lying across the bed, the back of her head blown off.

"What the fuck that nigga done went and done?" Wise shouted, looking anywhere he thought Domino might be hiding, but he was nowhere in sight.

"He's gone," Wise and Shiloh said in unison as they entered the room.

Shiloh watched Royal work to save Ascada. "Is she gon' be all right?"

"I don't know." Royal dug into Ascada's wounded side with a steak knife, trying to get the bullet out.

"Ahhhhhh, ouucccchhhhhh!" Ascada cried out, sweating, running a fever, and violently shaking.

"I need a needle and thick thread. Oh, and some scissors. Ascada, the only thing I can give you for pain is a shot of serum. I just don't know what it might do to you and the baby."

"Do it. Just save my baby."

"I'm going to save you too." Royal shot just a small amount of the serum into the wound. "Now you have to try and push this baby out. Mo, grab a leg. Emil, grab the other. Pepper, try and scoot behind her and push her back up."

Ascada screamed out in pain as Pepper scooted behind her, pushing her body and side into a fold.

Wise and Shiloh rushed back in with all the things Royal had asked for.

"Push, Ascada! Push hard!" Pepper chanted in her ear.

She grunted like a wild, wounded animal left for dead. "If-I-don't . . . ah, aha, ah . . . make . . . it . . . ooooooh . . . don't give my baby . . . Oh God . . . to my . . . mother!"

"Shhhhh! Use all your energy to push," Royal told her.

Pepper felt Ascada relax her body. "Push again!"

"I am!" Ascada screamed back.

"Push harder," Royal told her.

After an hour of pushing, Royal said, "One more big push, Ascada. Come on, the baby's head is crowning. "

"Oh shit!" Shiloh and Wise excitedly yelled as they saw a black hairy ball stretch open what used to look like a vagina.

Ascada pushed one last time, and the baby slipped out.

"It's a boy, Ascada, a boy!"

Royal spooned the baby's mouth with a plastic spoon, clearing his airway, and he began to cry. "He's beautiful. But we have to get him to the hospital. He's panting, struggling to breathe."

Knock, knock, knock!

"Housekeeping. Is everything all right?" a woman's voice asked through the door.

Wise answered the door then backed into the cottage, his hands held up in the air and a gun pointed to his face.

CHAPTER 69

Mo's excitement from the birth of Ascada's baby quickly faded as she looked toward the door. She looked around the room for some type of weapon. "Bitch, what are you doing here?" she asked angrily, feeling the pit of her stomach about to erupt.

"Hello, mommy dearest." Gabby pushed Wise in the chest with her .32 caliber pistol.

"How di—"

"Easy. Very easy. I paid a lot of money to find you."

"Where's my daughter?" Mo screamed. She slowly began to walk up on Gabby.

"You mean *my* daughter. How does Mya, Kennedy, Charlotte sound for her new name, to go along with her new life?"

Mo leaped at Gabby, but her shot was faster. She aimed to shoot her right between the eyes, but missed and hit her in the arm and leg.

Shiloh slowly began to reach around his back for his gun, and Pepper slid from behind Ascada to go and help Mo.

Royal continued to do CPR on the baby boy.

Gabby kicked at Pepper's head, only missing by half an inch. "Get your funky ass away from her."

The baby boy began to cry again, taking Gabby's attention, and Pepper dragged Mo to the wall.

Gabby peeped over at the small, squirming infant. "Well, well, well, what do we have here? Another worthless bastard?" She put her hand on her hip and shook the gun at the women, ranting like a wild woman. "You black, hot-between-the-legs bitches will never learn!"

Royal screamed at Gabby, "I need to get him to the hospital. His lungs are undeveloped."

"Let 'im die. He'll be better off. Matter of fact,"—Gabby pointed the gun at the baby—"I'll end his suffering right now. Rid the world of another problem."

Royal shielded the baby with her body.

"Why are you doing this? Just go away," Mo said as she crawled to the bathroom.

"Oh no, my ungrateful, lost child. And leave you alive, to try and take my new daughter? Never! That little girl is going to be the daughter I never had. I'm going to put her in all the top-notch schools, buy her the most expensive dresses, and teach her to use eloquent words and phrases."

Out the corner of her eye, Gabby saw Shiloh pulling the gun from his waist. *POW! POW!* She shot the wall beside and above his head, making him drop the gun. "Don't make me kill you. I need to plant these murders on you." Gabby laughed.

"Lady, who are you?"

"She's my evil, tormented mother."

Wise and Shiloh looked from the crazy white woman standing before them holding a gun down to the floor to the light-skinned wounded woman on the floor.

Ascada reached for her son, and Royal lay the small baby in her weak, shaking arms.

"Pepper, name him Prince," she said, her voice weak and faint. "Yes, Prince." She kissed sweet baby Prince on his forehead and lips then her body went limp.

Royal grabbed the baby before he tumbled to the floor and gave him to Pepper, then tried CPR several times before laying across Ascada's body, defeated.

"Ascada," she said, "I'm so, so sorry. Oh God!"

Gabby, tired of all the antics, yelled, "Y'all bitches, get on the ground execution-style."

Emil stood right in front of the gun. "You must be as crazy as you sound and look."

"And you must be one of the stupid ones." She slammed the gun across Emil's head, dropping her to the floor. "Y'all four, get face down." Gabby pointed her gun at the women. "You two, kneel down beside them."

Wise and Shiloh did as she said.

Gabby put on a pair of gloves and grabbed the guns that Wise and Shiloh had. *Pow!* She shot Emil in the back twice.

Pow! Pow! She shot Pepper and Royal in the back.

Pow! Pow! Pow! She shot Mo in the head, and twice in the back.

Wise screamed, "What the fuck, lady? Are you crazy?"

Gabby laughed like a mad woman. "No, you are. Why did you shoot these poor girls?" She emptied the clips and threw the guns to them.

Just as Gabby put her finger on the trigger and pointed the gun at the baby, someone whistling "Take Me Back to Dear Ol' Dixie" kicked in the door of the cottage.

"Why the fuck did you follow me here?"

Without saying a word, he raised his .45 mm and filled Gabby Cantrell's body from head to toe with bullets. Her body jerked from side to side like something out of *The Matrix*, until he ceased firing and her body hit the floor.

Wise and Shiloh untied the girls and checked their

pulses. Royal and Emil had faint ones, but they couldn't find one for Mo, nor Pepper.

The whistling man's heavy boots clunked on the hardwood floor as he walked over to Gabby's bullet-ridden body. He took out a big, sharp, shiny knife and stabbed her in the chest. "You know, we kinda in the same business. You fellas rob the rich and I kill 'em." He laughed a hearty laugh like he was having a regular coffee break conversation at work.

"I always considered myself a good person gone bad because of circumstances, but this here"—he dug out Gabby's heart like a butcher, and held it in the air—"jus' pure evil. Bad seed from birth"—and dropped it in a plastic freezer bag. Then he cut off her left hand and dropped it in the bag too. He began whistling a different tune.

Wise and Shiloh had did some real gansta shit in the past, but this was some true monster-type shit.

The baby began to cry.

"Well, my work here is done. Y'all, call the police and tell them that a baby's just been born and four women have been shot." He began whistling again, picked up Gabby's body up, threw it over his shoulder, and disappeared through the door like he'd never been there.

Wise and Shiloh grabbed their guns and duffle bags. They both kissed their lovers, whispering promises in their ears, encouraging survival, anonymously called the police, and reluctantly left the cottage.

CHAPTER 70

"Unbelievable . . . just unbelievable," Oprah said as she turned her attention from the large projector screen back to the yellow leather sofa. "One of the most miraculous things about this is how you all became friends and where it led you. How was it to find out that your best friend Royal had the only male child from your child's father?"

Mo and Royal resituated themselves in their seats, uncomfortable from the question. Mo gave Royal a look that said, "We are still going to deal with this."

"We've been through so much in the past year," Mo said, "that's the last thing on our mind."

Oprah asked her staff to bring out baby Prince. Then she said, "Pepper, how do you think being a mother is going to change your carefree lifestyle and hopes of becoming a singer?"

"He's been a joy to my life. I can still pursue a singing career and be a mother. I have a lot to teach him about people and life."

"Emil, how are you dealing with your new physical handicap?"

"I'm taking it one day at a time. My legs have some feeling, but my back is still weak. It's harder for my kids because I can't jump up and run with them or move as fast."

"Here's the two questions that have been so mind-boggling to me and my best girlfriend Gayle. Are the police and FBI working hard at finding your daughter Kemoni, and have you two,"—she pointed at Royal and Pepper—"seen or heard from the kidnappers?"

"Right now, the last place they have spotted Kemoni was in Kentucky. They seem to think Gabby Cantrell arranged for her ex-husband's daughter to get Kemoni if something were to happen to her."

Royal and Pepper both said no they had not spoken or seen their kidnappers, that they didn't even know their real names. They were smart not to leak any information because they knew the police and FBI were looking and listening to the interview.

Wise and Shiloh had whispered in their ear, the day they were shot, that when the police came to tell them that they indeed had been kidnapped and made to do all the robberies, so that they wouldn't be charged with anything.

"We would just like to say that we thank Nevada for saving us from Tonk, and she can get in contact with us through Jovan Mims. The kids need to stay in touch with their sister."

"Thank you, ladies, for your story. And the new book is on the way from The Clique. No title yet."

All of them hugged Oprah and left the set.

CHAPTER 71

As the women embraced and prepared to depart, Pepper saw Shiloh standing across the street. She pushed Emil's wheelchair to her limo and kissed her and Kaylen bye. Then she grabbed Royal's arm, just as she and King were getting into their limo. "Mo, watch King and Prince for a minute."

"What's wrong? Everything okay?"

Pepper motioned her head across the street toward Shiloh.

Royal held her swollen belly. The baby began to kick like she knew her daddy was there.

Royal and Pepper walked across the busy Chicago Street and stood in front of Shiloh.

"Is he all right?" Pepper asked. "I just wanna know if he's okay."

"Here." He handed Pepper a medium-size FedEx box. "Everything's in there."

"You need me to stay?" she asked Royal.

"No, I'm fine." Pepper walked back across the street.

Mo situated the boys in the limo and studied the beautifully wrapped package sitting on the seat. Was it from Jovan? She pulled the small card off: *This is to show how sorry I am for causing you so much trouble all your life.* It was signed Gabby Cantrell.

She unwrapped the box and folded back the pink tissue paper, to reveal Gabby Cantrell's heart and left hand. Worried her mother would come back to harm her, Mo took out the gun she carried in her purse, wrapped the package back up, and placed them in a trashcan next to the limo. She was finished with that chapter of her life.

Shiloh stared at Royal's huge belly. "That's my seed?"

She rubbed her swollen belly. "Yeah," she said, studying his disgusted eyes.

"Why you keep it?"

Surprised at his question and nasty attitude, she said, "What? Nigga, I ain't ask you for shit! I can take care of mine." She turned to walk back across the street.

King watched Shiloh grab his mother's arm and talk angrily to her. He balled up his fist, anger welling inside of him about his mother's sad face.

"Don't leave. We need to talk."

"You just asked me why I keep this baby, and you think I wanna sit around and shoot the shit with you?" Royal wiped the tears from her face.

"Everything I told you when we were together, I meant." He reached out and rubbed her belly with both hands.

"So how could you ask me that?" Royal put her hand on her back and looked toward the ground.

King wanted to jump out of the limo and punch the man that was making his mother cry in the mouth. He'd overheard her talking to his auntie and seen her cry so many nights about his father Spencer Mack. And now here she was crying again about another man.

"What if being with me meant something sinful?"

"What do you mean?"

Shiloh paced back and forth. "I mean, if me and you being together was an abomination, wrong, not suppose to be."

"I don't know. I love you. I want to be with you, no matter what."

Shiloh was trembling, nervous, upset. "And if this baby had some type of sickness or genetic disability, would you still want it?"

"Yes, she's my child. Our child."

"My father died and left me with a heavy burden to bear. Read this and then tell me if you still feel the same way."

Shiloh,

I've done such a poor job of raising you, told you so many lies, and hurt so many people in my lifetime. But you've always been a devoted son. You've raised me to be your dad. I learned so much from you. I know you think your robbing the dope man was the worst thing in the world for you to do, but I've done worse. You robbed to support my AIDS, something I didn't have to get, just being dick-headed. I raped someone when I was younger, the same time I was dealing with yo' mama, that's why she left me.

The woman I raped had a child, a girl, and she the one you brought to the house that day, Royal.

"Nooooooooo!" Royal dropped to the ground, holding her stomach.

King jumped out the limo, dug into the trashcan he saw Mo throw the gun in, and sprinted across the street to his mother. He pointed the gun at Shiloh. "Back off my mama!"

Shiloh, thinking it was a toy, reached for the gun and . . .